IN TIMES
OF TROUBLE

Refuge Book 1

P.M. Kuiper

REFORMED
FREE PUBLISHING
ASSOCIATION

Scripture cited is taken from the King James (Authorized) Version

Reformed Free Publishing
1894 Georgetown Center Drive
Jenison, MI 49428
www.rfpa.org
mail@rfpa.org

Cover design by Erika Kiel
Interior design by Katherine Lloyd / theDESKonline.com

ISBN: 978-1-959515-48-7
Ebook ISBN: 978-1-959515-49-4
LCCN: 2025931439

IN TIMES
OF TROUBLE

CHAPTER ONE

The Netherlands – Summer, 1846

Today is market day. Finally! My favorite day of the week.

I twist my hair into a braid and tuck it under my bonnet. In the kitchen, Mother sets out a pitcher of fresh milk and a tray of warm gingerbread. I eat a quick breakfast and head for the door.

Three-year-old Luc blocks my way. "Play with me."

I tousle his hair. "I can't. I have to help Father and Theo at the market."

"What's market?"

"It's where we sell our cheese."

"What's sell?"

He'll go on like this all day if no one stops him. I look to Mother for help.

She hands him a piece of gingerbread. "No more questions. Tess has to go."

Outside, the air is moist and gray. My brother Theo lugs wheels of cheese down to the canal, where our flat-bottomed boat awaits. He's fifteen, two years older than me. Father says he's a big help on the farm already. I say he's annoying. And ignorant. And rude. I could go on.

I ask him, "Where is Father?"

"Milking."

"Still? We don't want to be late to the market."

1

He lifts a wheel of cheese into the boat. "You don't care about the market. You just want to see your friends."

See what I mean? Annoying.

Not that he's wrong. With school out for the summer, I only see my friends at church and the market.

But Mother says it's good to have friends. Father too. I tell Theo, "Friends are important. The Bible says Jonathan and David were friends and Jonathan saved David's life. Wouldn't it be exciting to save someone's life? Would you save my life if the king wanted to kill me?"

"Hmmm." He rubs his chin. Like he can't make up his mind.

To be fair, it isn't likely the king will want to kill me. All I do is feed chickens, gather eggs, weed long rows of beans, and on market day, help sell Mother's cheese.

Father emerges from the barn, pulling on a clean apron. We climb into the canalboat and push away from the bank toward the town of Otten.

Mist hangs heavy on the canal. Gray, hazy barns peek out at us as Father poles past neighboring farms.

I pull my shawl closer. "Misty mornings are my favorite. They're so..."

"Quiet?" Theo offers. Like he's hoping it stays that way.

"Mysterious." I point to the shadowy outline of a windmill. "It's a giant, I think."

"Maybe if we're quiet, it'll leave us alone."

I have no interest in being left alone. I stand up and wave my hand over my head. "Good morning, giant!"

The boat rocks and Theo scowls at me. Father just smiles.

This is my first year going to market. I could have gone last year, but Mother needed my help with Luc. At least that's what she said. Sometimes she treats me like I'm still ten.

Theo's been going to market for years. He says sometimes, on the way home, Father sings. I hope this is one of those days.

He asks Father, "What was Uncle Ed upset about last night?"

Uncle Ed is Father's older brother. When he's upset, which is quite often, he comes to our house and talks with Father. I don't mind, because he usually brings Betsie with him. Betsie is my cousin and also my best friend.

Last night, Uncle Ed came without Betsie. And he stayed past dark. Which means he was *very* upset. Why? Because of our new minister at church. He told Father, "Rev. Bloem's preaching isn't Reformed. He preaches the wisdom of men instead of the Bible."

I know he said those things because I was listening in from the other room. Yes, I know it's rude to listen in on adult conversations. It's one of my worst faults. But Uncle Ed talks loud. And how else can I learn anything?

Father presses his lips together before answering Theo's question, like he's searching for the right words. "Uncle Ed wanted to discuss some church matters."

See what I mean? That's not an answer.

The motion of our boat sends V-shaped waves lapping at the banks of the canal. Soon our canal empties into a larger canal that flows past the pretty, red-tiled roofs of Otten.

Below the market square, Father ties our boat to the bank. He and Theo set up our booth while I sweep the area clean. I attach yellow and red streamers to the booth to catch the breeze while they unload cheese from the boat.

Other farmers and merchants arrive and set up their booths. The baker sets out dozens of golden-brown loaves. The butcher places dark slabs of beef on a clean white sheet. He stands by with his cleaver and scale.

On the far side of the square, there's a pen with goats, and another with suckling pigs. The odor is not pleasant. That's why we set up on *this* side of the square. But there are good smells too—coffee and tea and spices.

Mother doesn't buy spices from the market. Too expensive, she says. Those are for rich town folk. She grows the spices we need in our garden, mostly rosemary and sage.

Excitement spreads across the square as neighbors greet each other and prepare for the day. I work quickly so I'll have time to visit with my friends before the market opens.

Betsie is the first to arrive. She and Uncle Ed sell cabbage and turnips. Her mother died when she was a baby and Uncle Ed needs her help, so this is already her third year going to the market.

We're soon joined by other friends—Julia Jonkeer, Nellie Vogel, and Johannah Bos.

Julia is my best friend who *isn't* my cousin. She has dark eyes and long dark curls. I envy those curls. But she wishes she had straight blond hair like me, so I guess we're even.

Nellie sells flowers at the market. Johannah sells eggs. Julia doesn't have to sell anything. Her father is an elder in the church and an important man. But she comes to the market so she can visit with us.

She grasps my hand. "Have you seen my mother? She's going to have her baby any day now."

Betsie starts to giggle. Julia's been saying "any day now" for weeks.

Nellie says, "That reminds me," then claps a hand over her mouth. "But I'm not supposed to say."

We all wait to hear more. Nellie is good at lots of things. She can sing beautifully. She can arrange flowers into amazing bouquets. But she can't keep a secret to save her life. "It's my sister, Tina," she says. "The one who got married last summer. She's going to have a baby! But don't tell anyone."

Johannah claps her hands. "You'll be an aunt."

"I know. And I love babies."

Eva Everhart swishes up in a new calico skirt. She says, "*Everyone* loves babies." Like she's the expert.

I don't disagree. "They smell so good."

Betsie grins. "Except when they don't."

Everyone laughs. Everyone but Eva. Eva only laughs when *she* says something funny.

"I hope my mother has a girl," Julia says.

Eva puts her nose in the air. "Boys are *boring*. You can't even play dress-up with them."

"And besides," Julia says, "I already have three brothers."

I know how she feels. I'm also plagued with brothers. Luc drives me crazy with all his questions. And Theo, well, I already told you about him.

Eva twirls her new skirt in case we didn't notice.

I noticed, believe me. When it comes to clothes, I envy Eva. She always has nice things. She doesn't have to sell anything at the market either. Her father has a good government job.

Theo walks past, carrying a large wheel of cheese on his shoulder. My friends stop talking. Nellie smiles at him. Eva laughs and tosses her hair.

Fortunately, Theo is ignorant about girls.

Julia sighs and watches him go.

Betsie laughs.

I groan.

The tower clock chimes nine o'clock. Time for the market to open. We split up, and I take my place at our booth.

It's a busy morning. Everyone knows Mother's cheese is the best. It sells quickly. Father and Theo have to return to the boat to bring up more.

While they're away, the widow Wolters approaches. She wears an old gray top and a ragged skirt. She's shorter than I am and walks with a cane, but still she frightens me.

Mrs. Everhart, Eva's mother, arrives at the same moment. She frightens everyone. She pushes in front of the widow. "Be careful with that cane. You could trip someone."

The widow looks at her cane, then back at Mrs. Everhart. "Thank you. I hadn't thought of that."

There's mischief in her eyes. I have to hide my smile.

Mrs. Everhart doesn't say hello or even look at me. She pokes at the cheese and sniffs her disapproval. "We haven't had proper cheese since the Hofmans moved to Amsterdam."

I'd like to tell her what I think of that, but I don't want Father to think I can't handle difficult customers. Besides, no one in their right mind picks a fight with Mrs. Everhart.

The widow Wolters, who might be *out* of her right mind, says, "You mustn't settle for second-rate cheese. I suggest you go to the market in Amsterdam."

Mrs. Everhart ignores her. She buys a large wheel, all the while complaining about the price and quality. When she turns to go, she gives the widow a withering glare. The widow does not wither.

When Mrs. Everhart is gone, the widow steps forward, examines our cheese, and selects a small wheel. It has a dent in the side. Theo got careless, probably.

I offer her a different one, but she refuses to part with the one in her hand.

"But it has..."

"I know what it has."

She's hoping for a discount, and that's what I give her. Theo won't like it, but Father will approve. After all, she's a widow and poor.

By noon, the square begins to empty. We're happy with the day's sales. The money box is full. Father and Theo take down the booth while I pack up the remaining cheese for the trip home.

After the market closes, the men gather to visit on the steps in front of the church. Most of them are farmers like Father, with square shoulders, sun-weathered faces, and simple clothing. Nearly all wear a black cap.

I look for my friends but can't find them in the press of people.

It's July now and getting hot, so I position myself in the shade of a sycamore tree. From there I can listen in on the men without being noticed. I know, rude. I explained about that earlier.

Father shakes hands with the other men and greets them by name. "Good afternoon, Willem. Hello, Peter. How are you, Dirk?" They respond in friendly terms. Everyone likes Father. Uncle Ed is there too. He's easy to spot, as he stands a head taller than most of the others.

The men discuss the weather, wondering how the heat will affect the crops. I'm not especially interested in farm talk.

Mr. Everhart arrives. He's Eva's father and magistrate over Otten and all the surrounding countryside. He wears a tall black hat, a bulging waistcoat, and a fine linen shirt with a purple cravat. The men part as he makes his way to the top step.

Mr. Jonkeer follows close behind, as if connected by an invisible string. He's Julia's father and an elder at church. He wears a similar hat and waistcoat and positions himself one step below Mr. Everhart.

Father and the other men doff their caps in deference to the wealthy and important leaders. Talk dies down while they wait to hear what the two men will say.

Mr. Everhart speaks first. "Another successful market day. If there's a finer market in all of the Netherlands, I haven't seen it."

"Yes. Yes." Everyone agrees.

"And no finer town than Otten."

"Indeed. No finer town."

"And no finer church." Mr. Jonkeer gestures to the church building behind him.

"Yes. Yes."

"And now," he adds, "we have a pastor who understands the natural potential of our people. Rev. Bloem studied divinity in Paris. He has degrees in philosophy and French literature."

Mr. Everhart nods in agreement. "It speaks well of our town, that a man of his stature is willing to lead us in matters of religion."

Mr. Jonkeer's face beams at Mr. Everhart's approval. His chest nearly bursts through his waistcoat.

I'm not especially interested in church talk either. But a new edge in Mr. Jonkeer's voice gets my attention. "We have *one* Reformed church in Otten. You've heard of troublemakers in other towns, starting new churches, not part of the state-approved church, mind you. These churches are free of government control."

Last night, Uncle Ed talked with Father about the new churches too. He used those same words, "free of government control." But he said it like it was a *good* thing.

Mr. Jonkeer's voice is tinged with anger as he continues. "These new churches are a disgrace. Something must be done."

I watch Father, wondering what he's thinking.

Uncle Ed steps forward. "I say the *state* church is a disgrace." No one ever has to wonder what Uncle Ed is thinking. He says, "It's the new churches that are faithful to the Bible and the Reformed confessions."

Mr. Jonkeer eyes him coolly. "That's *your* opinion."

"It's true. Some of their leaders learned their catechism from Rev. Bolthouse."

Rev. Bolthouse was our old pastor. Father and Mother loved him. I thought everyone did. I found out later, after he died, that some people *didn't*. They said he was old-fashioned.

Mr. Jonkeer smirks at Uncle Ed. "Ah, yes, old Rev. Bolthouse." His voice is full of scorn.

Some of the men laugh.

Uncle Ed scowls at them. "He taught us the faith. Are we not thankful for that?"

No one responds.

Mr. Jonkeer smiles with satisfaction. "There are more important things than knowing the catechism. We need sermons that are relevant today, sermons that open our minds to new ways of thinking, that help us become a great nation. That's what Rev. Bloem brings."

Mr. Everhart holds up a hand, making clear he will have the last word. "Be assured of one thing. We will not allow these new churches in Otten. Not while I'm magistrate."

Having said what he came to say, he strides back through the crowd. Mr. Jonkeer scurries after him, like a shadow not wanting to be left behind.

Talk among the men slowly turns back to crops and weather.

I stop listening and make my way back toward the canal.

Julia appears at my side. "Did you hear what Betsie's father said?"

Before I can answer, Eva joins us. "Why would Betsie's father defend those bad churches? My father says he's a radical."

I don't respond. To be honest, I'm not sure what "radical" means. I'm not sure Eva does either.

"My father is a judge," she says, "so he should know." She turns to Julia. "You agree, don't you?"

That's just like Eva. She always tries to get Julia on her side.

Today, Julia resists. "He can't be *that* bad. He's Betsie's father."

Eva doesn't give up. "Our teacher said it's wicked to leave the church."

It's true, he did say that. I don't think Uncle Ed is wicked, but our teacher can't be wrong. It's confusing.

"Julia!" Mr. Jonkeer calls her from across the square.

She sighs. "Sorry. I have to go. I'll see you Sunday."

Eva hurries after Julia, still complaining about Uncle Ed.

Back at the canal, Theo is leaning against a tree, whittling a piece of wood. I ask him, "Did you hear the men talking?"

"Yeah."

"Did you hear what Uncle Ed said?"

"Yeah."

That's all. No comment. No opinion. Never even takes his eyes off his whittling. So helpful.

Soon Uncle Ed and Betsie join us. Uncle Ed looks serious, but then he always looks serious. He sees Father approaching and says, "We need to talk."

Father shakes his head. "Not here. Not now."

"Tomorrow, then."

"Alright."

Back in our canalboat, Father guides us away from the bank. I remember what Theo told me before. Sometimes, on the way home from the market, Father sings. This is not one of those days.

CHAPTER TWO

Thursday, I rise early and do my chores—feed the chickens, gather eggs, and weed two rows of beans. With my work done, I go for a walk out past the barley fields.

A breeze rustles through the long grass, a welcome relief from this week's heat. Birds sing from the reeds. Squirrels chase each other in the trees. I begin to run. I do that when I'm happy. During the school year, my friends and I race almost every day.

I go as far as a grove of pine trees about halfway to Betsie's house. Today I promised to watch Luc while Mother makes a batch of cheese, so I circle the pines and turn back toward home. As I return to our farmyard, a shaft of sunlight breaks through the clouds. It frames our house in a stream of golden light, like something out of a fairy story.

Not that our house is a castle. It's small for five people. It's painted white, with blue shutters. Petunias fill the window boxes and spill over the sides.

Along one side of the house, Father has built a shed. That's where Mother makes her cheese. It has its own cookstove and lots of wooden presses. The walls inside are lined with shelves filled with wheels of aging cheese.

Mother says that after my next birthday, I can begin to help her make cheese. That used to seem a long way off, but it isn't anymore. It's only three weeks away, the last day of July.

Our kitchen has a cookstove and a table for eating. The walls are decorated with ceramic plates and tiles from Delft that came to us when Grandmother died.

Everything in the house is neat and tidy. Except my room, which is always a mess. It's one of my worst faults.

Our barn has a stall for our horse, Samson, and more stalls for Madam Maas and the other milking cows. Why do we call Samson, Samson? Because he's uncommonly strong. Why Madam Maas? Father says she's like the Maas River, big and slow, and never in a hurry to get anywhere.

Samson is my best friend who *isn't* a person. He nickers when he sees me, and sometimes I bring him apples from the cellar. I don't love cows in general or Madam Maas in particular, but I have to share my barn with them. Mother couldn't make cheese without them.

The barn has a ladder that leads to a loft, which is filled with secret places where a girl can be alone when she needs to get away from annoying brothers.

Actually, Theo used to play in the loft too. But now he thinks he's too old for that. Too bad for him.

When I say *our* house and *our* barn, what I mean is, Mr. Borgman's house and barn. Mr. Borgman owns the land we farm and even the house we live in. He owns other farms too. His father owned them before him, and his children will own them when he's gone.

The Netherlands is a small country and rich people own all the land. So people like Father have to work for them and pay them most of the profits. Theo could tell you more. He complains about it all the time.

I watch Luc in the morning while Father and Theo work the fields and Mother tends to her cheese. We all gather at midday for a big dinner. In the afternoon I practice my arithmetic and study my catechism while Father and Theo return to the fields. We gather again in the evening for a light supper.

Later, we walk across the fields to Betsie's house. Often on Thursday evenings, Uncle Ed invites us over for a sort of midweek worship service. He calls it a conventicle.

I don't mind, because I get to spend time with Betsie, which is always fun. I only wish my other friends could come. I asked Uncle Ed once if I could invite Julia. He said, "No, the Jonkeers would not be interested."

Tonight Mr. and Mrs. Koster come. And the Vissers and the Bloks, with their young families.

Chairs are reserved for adults, so Betsie and I sit on the floor.

Uncle Ed opens his Bible to begin but stops when another family arrives. The Huizens are a young couple who live up the lane from us. They're the nicest people ever.

Father motions to Theo, who leaps to his feet and disappears out the back door. A moment later he appears at the window.

"I'm sorry." Mrs. Huizen looks embarrassed. "Is that really necessary?"

"Better safe than sorry," Mother says. "It's the law."

Mother explained the law to me the first time this happened. When Napoleon conquered the Netherlands, he made it illegal for more than twenty people to gather in one place without approval of the government. He meant to keep Dutch citizens from rebelling against French rule.

Napoleon is gone now, and the Netherlands is an independent nation, but the government uses that old law to stop people from forming new churches, even from meeting to worship in their own homes. With the Huizens, we number twenty-one, so Theo has to listen from the window.

Mrs. Huizen sighs. "It seems silly."

"Perhaps," Mother says. "But we don't want trouble. If the constable comes, he'll find us peacefully and *lawfully* gathered."

Betsie and I turn our eyes to the door. If anyone else arrives, *we'll* be allowed to listen from the window.

But no one else comes.

Uncle Ed begins the service. He reads from 2 Corinthians 11, where Paul says that five times he was whipped, three times he was beaten, once he was stoned, and three times he suffered shipwreck.

"What's shipwreck?" Luc asks.

Betsie starts to giggle.

I clap a hand over Luc's mouth. It isn't so bad that he asked a question. He's only three. And it isn't really church.

Uncle Ed keeps reading. Paul faced perils of waters, perils of robbers, perils by his own countrymen, perils by the heathen, perils in the city, perils in the wilderness, perils in the sea.

"What's perils?" Luc asks.

Betsie bursts into giggles again.

Uncle Ed ignores her and turns to Father. "Everyone who follows Jesus must be prepared to suffer."

He reads more Bible verses and explains them to us. He isn't a minister, just a farmer like Father, but he finished high school. I listen carefully to see if he says anything "radical."

He says our old nature is dead in sin because of Adam, but now we have new life in Jesus. That isn't radical. It's in the Bible. He says we need to know how great our sins are, and how we can be set free from them, and how we can thank God for setting us free. That isn't radical either. It's in the catechism.

Luc hates to sit still. Tonight he's even more of a distraction than usual. First he wants to sit by Mother, then Father, then Mother again. He whimpers and fusses and sobs.

Betsie and I take him into the kitchen so the adults can listen. At first he's alright, but then he starts bawling like a baby.

Mrs. Huizen joins us. She's tall and pretty, with blue eyes and golden hair. She pulls a square of candy from her pocket.

Luc stops crying.

She gives him a bite. "Are you girls enjoying your summer holiday?"

"Yes," I say. "But we miss seeing our friends every day."

She smiles. "It seems like only yesterday when I was in school."

"Did you run races?"

"Oh, yes. But I was better at short ones. Across the schoolyard and back."

"It's the same with me," Betsie admits. "If it's longer than a sprint, I have to hope someone twists an ankle or something. But Tess can run and run."

I elbow her for embarrassing me. I *do* like to run, but Julia still beats me half the time.

Luc starts bawling again, and even candy doesn't help.

Mother joins us and takes him outside. Mrs. Huizen returns to her husband's side. Betsie and I return to our places.

Uncle Ed is finishing his talk. Thanks to Luc, I'll never know if he said anything radical or not. He says, "Let's sing. Who wants to suggest a psalm?"

I raise my hand, then drop it again. Which should I choose? Psalm 1 is my favorite. But so is 100. And 42. And 116. And 124.

"Psalm 23!" Betsie just blurts it out. She doesn't even raise her hand.

But I have only myself to blame. I have too many favorites. And I hate to choose. It's one of my worst faults. And to be honest, Psalm 23 is also my favorite.

After we sing, Uncle Ed closes with prayer. The Vissers and Bloks, who have small children, leave for their homes. Betsie and I head to the kitchen to prepare coffee and pastries for the adults who remain. Mrs. Huizen joins us and asks how she can help. Did I mention that she's one of the nicest people ever? Why can't everyone be like that?

She pours coffee while Betsie and I plate pastries. We're starting to pass them out when Uncle Ed says, "We can start a new Reformed church, right here in Otten. Free from government control."

I trade looks with Betsie. A new church? When would we see our friends? School doesn't meet again until September.

But Uncle Ed isn't done. "Maybe we can start a Christian school too."

I nearly drop my platter. If he gets his way, we'll *never* see our friends. He's trying to ruin everything.

But Father isn't convinced. "Six families don't make much of a church."

"Other towns have done it. Drogeham, Hattem, and now Wittemeer."

"Yes, but they're struggling. They're small and poor."

"Is *that* what concerns you? Money?"

Father presses his lips together. "Their leaders have been fined thousands of guilders. Some have been put in prison. Yes, that concerns me."

Uncle Ed dismisses Father's concern with a wave of his hand. "That's why I read about Paul's troubles. Followers of Christ must be willing to face opposition."

"Yes, but we're just a few families. We don't even have a place to meet."

"I thought..." Uncle Ed hesitates, "we could use your barn."

I stare at him. Church in our barn? With Madam Maas and the cows?

"No." Father's voice is firm. "Everything at my place belongs to Mr. Borgman. You know that. I'm just a caretaker."

Uncle Ed scoffs at that. "When was the last time he stepped foot on the place? He doesn't need to know."

Father shakes his head. "I won't take advantage of his trust."

For anyone else, that would be the end of the conversation, but not Uncle Ed. He says, "We'll find another place. We'll worship in a field if we have to."

In a field! I wait for someone to tell him how horrid that would be. No one does.

Theo is still at the window. He can hear everything they say. About having church in a field. But he's too busy winding a blade of grass around his finger to notice.

Mr. Huizen speaks up. "Abby and I have talked about this, and we're not ready to leave the state church. It has weaknesses, we recognize that. But we think it's better to stay and work to reform it."

"You're just afraid," Uncle Ed says. "That's all."

I feel bad for Mr. Huizen. Uncle Ed may not be a radical, but he sure can be rude.

He turns to Father and Mother. "Our children need to learn their catechism."

"They *do* learn their catechism," Mother says.

That's true. Even though Rev. Bloem doesn't require it, Theo and I have to learn our catechism every week.

Uncle Ed sighs. "Maybe it's too soon to form our own church. But I've been thinking about traveling to Wittemeer on Sunday to worship with the new church there. Join me in that, at least."

Mrs. Koster glances at her husband. "We've been discussing doing the same thing. Until we can form a new church in Otten."

Mother looks worried. "Wittemeer is so far."

"It's only an hour away," Uncle Ed says. "We travel there for business. Why not for worship?"

Father sets down his coffee. "I can't be away from home the whole day. Who will feed and water my animals? The cows must be milked, even on the Sabbath."

I smile inside. I knew the cows would come in useful someday.

"If it will help," Mr. Huizen says, "I can stop by and look after your animals."

My smile disappears. Why do the Huizens have to be so nice?

"Thank you, but no," Father says. "We won't go anywhere until I've had a chance to talk to Rev. Bloem. And the elders."

IN TIMES OF TROUBLE

I breathe a sigh of relief. Uncle Ed can't push Father around. Father will explain the problem to Rev. Bloem and the elders. And together, they'll find a solution. I go back to passing out pastries. I make sure Uncle Ed gets the smallest piece.

CHAPTER THREE

Sunday morning, I dress for church and braid my hair. I'm still worried Uncle Ed might have talked Father and Mother into going to church in Wittemeer. At breakfast, I pray that God will help them know which church to go to. And that it will be the one in Otten.

Either way, my Sunday outfit is a disappointment. I've been growing out of it for months. Mother promised to make me a new Sunday dress from cloth she bought this spring. It will be yellow, like an early ear of corn, with blue buttons. But it isn't finished yet.

After breakfast, Father leads us out into the lane and turns toward Otten. What a relief. A normal Sunday. At my own church. With all my friends.

The day is warm. Wheat fields shimmer in the sunlight. Starlings swirl overhead. We walk in the grass at the edge of the lane to avoid kicking up dust.

Father tells Mother, "Don't wait for me after church. I have to stay for a bit."

She nods that she understands.

I understand too. He's staying to talk with Rev. Bloem and the elders. I get permission to stay after church, too, and walk home with Father. More time to spend with my friends.

Knowing what Uncle Ed is trying to do, I decide to say something nice about our church. "I just love the way the church bell tower soars over the whole town. It's very majestic."

"What's 'jestic?" Luc asks.

"Stately," I say.

"What's stately?"

"Stuffy," Theo says. "That means it's too hot in the summertime."

"Oh."

Father chuckles. "And too cold in the winter. I can't argue with that."

"With hard benches in all seasons," Theo adds.

Even Mother laughs.

Theo! Why does he have to be so ignorant?

I try again. "It's pretty, though. The stone steps and high windows. And in the morning, the sun turns the brick all orange and gold."

Father isn't even paying attention. He holds his songbook in one hand and struggles to keep hold of Luc with the other.

It doesn't matter. He'll talk to Rev. Bloem and the elders. They'll make everything right.

A half hour walk brings us to Otten. We cross the canal using the White Bridge. The sections nearest the banks are made of brick, as orange as the royal crest. The section in the middle is wood and painted pure white, like a stork's head and shoulders. And it's a drawbridge, so the middle can be raised to let tall boats through and lowered to let people cross over.

Church members fill the streets—old men walking with canes, young fathers and mothers carrying babies, sisters holding hands. I glance at Theo, who's scratching his belly. If only I had a sister.

As we approach church, a couple of older boys round the corner of the building at a full gallop. I recognize them at once. Maarten Borgman and Max Everhart. They see Father and pull up sharply.

A moment later another boy rounds the corner. His yellow hair gleams in the sunlight. Xander Bloem, the minister's son.

"Ha!" shouts Xander, as he passes the others. Too late, he notices my family. He tries to pull up, but loses his footing and stumbles in front of Mother.

Father reaches out a hand to catch him, dropping his songbook in the effort.

Xander retrieves the songbook and hands it to Father. "Sorry... thank you...sorry."

Father releases his arm. "Are you alright?"

"I'm fine." He looks at Mother. "Sorry." He turns and rejoins the others, grinning as if to say, "Why didn't you warn me?" Together, they slip away, joking and jostling each other.

Inside church, Father and Theo take off their caps and place them on hooks. Father pauses to chat with an older couple.

I take the opportunity to observe what the older girls are wearing. Janna Schaaf has a new pair of white gloves, very nice. Anna van Dyke wears a maroon dress with a pattern of gold vines. My own drab skirt and top do not draw attention. I'm like the little ash girl in the story Grandmother used to tell. No prince would ever notice me.

Mother gives me a look. The one that says, "We don't come to church to admire the latest fashions."

I know I shouldn't care about such things. It's one of my worst faults.

When it's time to sit, I lead my family into church, turning into the first open row. At the same time, from the other aisle, Mrs. Bloem, the minister's wife, directs her family into the same row.

Xander and I meet in the middle. Xander looks at me with a sheepish grin and sits down beside me. I squeeze closer to Mother, putting Luc on my lap to make more room. I keep my eyes straight forward.

Other families file into church. Mrs. Jonkeer, looking very pregnant, marches her family down the center aisle. Julia gives me a quick wave as she passes.

The Everharts, looking like royalty in their beautiful suits and dresses, make their way to their usual spot in the third row, near the furnace and just below a sunlit window. No one else is allowed to sit in that row. The Everharts made a large contribution to the church to reserve that row for their family.

The Borgmans take another reserved row. All the rich families do the same. Mrs. Borgman wears a shimmering blue dress, but her face is pinched and pale. Maarten, pampered and soft around the middle, is still breathing hard from charging around the churchyard.

Mr. Borgman settles into his seat, examining the rest of the congregation. His bushy eyebrows rise and fall as he nods at fellow businessmen and scowls at everyone else.

Theo says Mr. Borgman is rude to Father and other farmers. He could tell you more about that. What bothers me is they don't even seem to enjoy their wealth and privilege. No one wears a sour face like Mrs. Borgman.

I soon regret my decision to put Luc on my lap. He refuses to sit quietly. He wiggles and fusses and whimpers.

"Sit straight," I whisper, just loud enough for him to hear.

"What's straight?" he answers, loud enough for the whole church to hear.

Mother takes over, but she can't keep him quiet either. She scoops him up, along with her shawl and his blanket, and takes him out so he won't disrupt worship.

Rev. Bloem enters the room, followed by the elders. He shakes Mr. Jonkeer's hand and steps behind the pulpit. He begins the service with prayer, then announces the opening song. I reach for my songbook. It isn't there! Mother must have accidentally taken it when she scooped up Luc.

I'm not sure what to do. I know lots of psalms by heart, but Rev. Bloem has chosen one of the new hymns.

Suddenly a songbook appears in front of me. Xander keeps his eyes forward but leans over so I can read it.

So embarrassing. I wish I'd stayed home. No, I wish he'd stayed home.

To my surprise, he sings beautifully, with a fine, clear voice. Who would have guessed?

Near the end of the first stanza, as we're singing about the birds of the air, Xander squeezes the songbook so that its covers flap open and shut. Like a bird. I try hard not to react. Is he doing it on purpose?

The next stanza mentions sailors on the sea. The songbook begins to rise and fall like waves of the ocean. I bite my lip and look away so he can't see my face. I've never been so relieved to have a song come to an end.

When Rev. Bloem begins his sermon, I listen to see if he says anything wrong. He talks about God and Jesus. He talks about Israel and the Netherlands. He talks about doctors and lawyers. I try to think what Uncle Ed said was wrong with his sermons but can't remember.

Beside me, Xander leans forward, putting his forehead on the bench in front of him. Then he slouches back. He lifts one leg over the other. Then he switches legs. It's as bad as sitting next to Theo.

Mother returns with Luc asleep on her shoulder and the missing songbook in her hand. What a relief. When the service ends, I sing the closing song with her. It's a good thing too. The song mentions thunder and lightning. I hate to think what Xander is doing with that.

After church, Betsie finds me in the corner of the churchyard. Other girls join us—Julia, Nellie, Susannah, and Gertie.

Julia says, "Did you see my mother? She's going to have her baby any day now."

Betsie starts to giggle.

We all agree that it certainly seems so.

"Xander is sweet on Tess." Nellie's grin reveals her chipped front tooth.

The other girls giggle in agreement. Nellie says, "Did you see how he shared his songbook with her?"

Yes. They saw. I decide not to tell them about the flapping bird and rolling seas.

Eva joins us. She turns her head this way and that, so we can see her new bonnet from every angle. "It's the latest style, with lace in front *and* on the sides."

Julia says, "We should meet at the schoolhouse tomorrow. We can run races or play shuffleboard."

Nellie says, "I can't."

"Why not?"

"Oh! I'm not supposed to say." She covers her mouth, even pinching her eyes shut, but the words simply must come out. "My mother takes in cleaning now. I'm supposed to help."

Eva shudders. "Clean other people's things? How horrid."

"I can't make it either," I say. "I have chores, and then I have to help with Luc."

Eva sighs dramatically. "You're just afraid I'll beat you at shuffleboard."

I've *never* lost to Eva at shuffleboard, but before I can remind her of that, Mr. Jonkeer appears. He tells Julia to gather up her little brothers and head home with her mother.

Soon all my friends are heading home with their families, but I stay behind at church. Father is meeting with Rev. Bloem and the elders this morning.

It's nearly noon, and the sun is getting hot. I decide to wait in the church's lower level, which stays cooler. And the room where the elders meet happens to be down there too.

CHAPTER FOUR

As soon as I reach the lower level of the church, I hear voices coming from the elders' meeting room. Rev. Bloem says, "I urge our members to love their neighbor. Even unbelievers. I think that's important."

"That *is* important," Father says, "but it can't replace the gospel. We're sinners. We need to hear about forgiveness, about God's grace."

Rev. Bloem starts to respond, but Mr. Jonkeer interrupts. "You sound like an ignorant peasant, Theodore. I want to think better of you."

"I do talk about Jesus," Rev. Bloem says. "I try to bring him into my sermon each week."

"But not the cross. Not that he's the son of God come to save us from our sins. Only what a good example he was."

"He *was* a good example."

"You can't cling to old ideas, Theodore." Mr. Jonkeer speaks impatiently, as if to a child. "We have a new message. A message for today."

"We need the gospel today."

"Times change. We have to change too. Have you even heard of the Enlightenment? We don't want to be thought of as ignorant. Uneducated."

"Education doesn't conflict with the gospel," Father says. "Not if it's proper education. The truth doesn't change."

"I'll tell *you* the truth." Mr. Jonkeer is angry now. "Your brother Ed is a troublemaker. We hoped you'd be more reasonable."

A footstep sounds behind me and a voice whispers, "You shouldn't listen in when the elders are meeting."

Startled, I turn around. There stands Xander Bloem. He drags a hand through his mop of yellow hair. "That's supposed to be private."

"Well...you shouldn't race around before church. You..." I turn and march across the room and up the stairs.

He follows me. "What are they talking about?"

"It's private."

"Come on."

"I don't know."

"Yes, you do. And so do I."

I spin around and face him. "Tell me, if you know so much."

"Your uncle wants to start one of those new churches. He wants your family to join him."

"You don't know what you're talking about."

"I do. I heard Mr. Jonkeer telling my father. He says your uncle is the problem. Your father is just going along."

"You shouldn't..." I want to accuse him of listening in but stop short. Tears threaten, but I will them to stop.

He steps closer, but I jerk away. If he puts a hand on my shoulder, if he says one thing, I'll have to punch him.

Footsteps sound on the stairs below. I wipe my face with my sleeve. A moment later, Father appears. "Hello, Xander. Hi, Tess."

"Hello," mumbles Xander.

We walk out of church. Xander turns one way. Father and I turn the other.

All the way home, I wait for Father to bring up his talk with Rev. Bloem and the elders. He doesn't say a word.

That leaves me to wonder. Is it true what they said? Is Uncle Ed a troublemaker? Is Father just going along? And if so, how can I help him to be more reasonable?

Back at home, I raid Mother's sewing basket for scraps of colored cloth and resume work on a rag doll, a present for Julia's mother's soon-to-be baby. I dress her in blue gingham, with long yellow yarn for hair. She's very pretty. I call her Lizbet.

Theo knocks on my door, which is half open. He looks around my room. "What a mess."

See what I mean? Rude. Not that he's wrong. Last year's school supplies are piled in one corner, yesterday's clothes in another.

He notices Lizbet. "What's with the doll?"

"It's for Mrs. Jonkeer's new baby. What do you want?"

"Nothing. Mother wants you in the kitchen."

He turns to go, but I stop him. "Do you think Uncle Ed is a troublemaker?"

"What? No. Why would you say that?"

"Mr. Jonkeer thinks he is. Because he wants to start one of those new churches."

"How do you know what Mr. Jonkeer thinks?"

"I...Never mind that. He just does."

"So?"

"It just makes me wonder. Why are they starting new churches? I wish I knew more about them."

"Me too." He lowers his voice. "I did hear one thing, though."

"What?"

"Some of them are talking about leaving the Netherlands. Going to America."

"Leaving the Netherlands? That just *proves* they're wrong."

"Not necessarily."

"Yes. Necessarily."

He disagrees. "The government put their ministers in prison. Elders and deacons too."

"That proves they're bad. The government wouldn't put *good* ministers in prison."

"Ha! Don't be ignorant."

I glare at him. That's hard to take—being called ignorant by Theo.

He doesn't seem to notice my glare. "In America they don't put ministers in prison."

"I don't care."

"They have other advantages too."

"No." I cross my arms. "They don't."

"They have lots of land. If someone is strong and willing to work, they can earn enough to buy their own land. Father could be like Mr. Borgman."

"Mr. Borgman is old and fat. And he has bushy eyebrows."

"And he's rich."

"Who wants to be rich? I don't. I'll never leave the Netherlands."

Theo sighs. "Father won't either. But I might."

"Theo! How could you?"

"I'm tired of rich people looking down on us. They walk around like they own everything. They wear expensive clothes and get the best houses. Even in church, they get the best seats, and we have to take whatever is left."

"Who cares about that? I love our farm."

"It isn't even *our* farm. Our house isn't even *our* house. It all belongs to Mr. Borgman. Father works all day, worries about the weather, prays for a good harvest, and Mr. Borgman is the one who gets rich."

"Father doesn't complain."

Theo snorts in frustration. "Maybe he should."

I don't want to hear any more about it. I take my doll and head to the kitchen to find Mother.

She's adding potatoes to a stewpot. We grow potatoes in a large plot beyond the canal and eat them with every meal. She smiles when she sees Lizbet. "How pretty."

28

"She's for the Jonkeers' new baby. I'm going to give her to Julia at church tonight."

"Oh." Mother glances at Father.

He rises stiffly from his chair and puts a hand on my shoulder. "Let's go for a walk."

This can't be good. The last time Father suggested we go for a walk, I was eight years old, and he told me Grandmother had died.

Outside, the afternoon air feels thick and heavy. The grass bends over with the weight of it. Father waits until we're well down the lane, then says, "We've decided not to go to church in Otten tonight."

"We can't not go to church."

"Of course. We're going to visit the new church in Wittemeer."

"But you told Uncle Ed—"

"I know. But I spoke with Rev. Bloem and the elders this morning. They're not going to change."

I can see that *he's* not going to change either. But I have questions. "Does the church in Wittemeer meet in a barn? With cows?"

He chuckles. "They have a building. No cows in church."

"Will Betsie be there?"

"Yes."

"And the Huizens?"

"Not the Huizens. But the Kosters will come. And the Vissers."

"And the Jonkeers? Will Julia be there?"

"No."

"Nellie?"

He kneels down, putting his face close to mine. "None of your other friends will be there. But the truth of God's word will be there. And that's the important thing."

I nod like I understand. But when we return home, I shut myself in my room. Not because I'm crying. I'm not crying. I just want to be alone. I sit on my bed and hold Lizbet on my lap. I tell her what I can't tell Father. "Friends are important too. They're important to me."

CHAPTER FIVE

By the middle of the afternoon, Father is in the barn, hitching Samson to our wagon. Soon we're on our way to Wittemeer.

Mother sits up front with Father. She says, "It's a fine day. See how the sunlight shimmers on the fields of wheat?"

Theo leans forward. "I've never been to Wittemeer. What's it like?"

"They're known for their horses," Father says. "Big ones. Belgians."

Theo sits up and scans the fields. "I hope we see some."

I hate all this talk of big horses and beautiful days. They're trying to make this into an adventure. Someone has to remind them how horrid it is. "It's such a long way."

Mother smiles. "But who doesn't like a wagon ride?"

I try again. "Just wait until winter, though."

"Winter?" Theo looks at me like I'm out of my right mind. "It's July."

"I'm just saying, it won't be so fun making this journey come December, when the lane is filled with snow and ice."

"Hey!" he says. "We could take the sleigh."

Mother's eyes light up. "Oh, a sleighride sounds like fun."

I glare at Theo, but he just grins. Ignorant. He's smart enough to run the farm when Father is away, but he can't translate a perfectly good glare.

Eventually the fields give way to homes, then shops and stores. I sit up at the sight of the Wittemeer church building. It's beautiful—taller than our church in Otten, with high arching windows and a soaring bell tower.

Father drives up to it. Then past it.

"Wait." I turn around. "We missed it."

He keeps going. "That's the state church."

We keep moving, leaving the beautiful church behind. Three blocks later, we round a corner and come to a halt.

I look around. "Where's the church?"

Father points to a sad-looking squat gray building.

My heart sinks. "That's not a church."

"A church isn't a building," Mother says. "It's a gathering of God's people, wherever they meet."

I know that, but still, it would be less confusing if they gathered in a church.

Father climbs down from the wagon and ties Samson to a post. "This building is all they can afford right now."

"But there are no people. Where is everybody?"

"Be patient." He glances up and down the lane. "We're early."

Soon another wagon appears, stopping on the other side of the street. It's Uncle Ed.

Betsie waves to me, and I ask Mother, "Can I go wait with her?"

"No."

"Can she wait with us?"

"No."

"Why not?"

"Shh."

Several minutes pass, and nothing happens. "Maybe no one else is coming."

"Be patient."

I've never been patient. She knows that. It's one of my worst faults. "If we turn back now, we can maybe still get back to our own church on time."

She gives me a look. The one that says, "That's enough."

At last a man arrives on foot and unlocks the door. Uncle Ed and Father approach him. They shake hands and enter the building.

Theo moves to the edge of his seat, ready to bolt. "*They* went in."

Mother shakes her head.

Finally, Father emerges from the building and returns to the wagon. He helps Mother down. I help Luc.

At the door, Mother straightens her skirt. She tells Theo to stand up straight. I check my braid and retie my bonnet. Then we all go inside.

The room is plain—a dozen rows of wooden benches facing a raised pulpit. The windows are small. Shelves line the walls, filled with wooden staves, iron hoops, and half-constructed barrels.

Betsie and I are allowed to sit together.

The Kosters arrive and sit with the Vissers. One by one, other families arrive. The men wear dark suits, mostly rumpled and worn. The women wear plain skirts of gray or blue, not very fashionable. None of the wealthier women have arrived yet.

There are some small children, but only one girl who looks to be my age. She has bright blue eyes and the tightest blond curls. Our eyes meet and she gives me a quick smile.

I also spot a longish-haired boy, not much older than me. He sits all alone in the back row. Curious. He catches me looking at him, and I quickly turn away.

What I don't see are the latest fashions. No elegant shoes. No glittering jewelry. I whisper to Betsie, "Where are the wealthy women?"

"I know," she says. "An entire church of poor people." Then, with a giggle, "Well, not poor, just...like us."

A minister and three elders enter the room. The minister climbs up behind the pulpit. His name is Rev. Hoek. He's tall and slender, and younger than Rev. Bloem. He opens the service by asking us to sing Psalm 100. My favorite!

He reads from Genesis 3, which tells how sin entered into the world, how the devil tempted Adam and Eve to disobey God.

Sometimes, in my real church, I let my mind wander during the sermon. It isn't that I'm not interested. I'm just easily distracted. Especially when I notice someone with a new dress. But it's easy to listen to Rev. Hoek. He talks about the garden and the trees and the snake and his sneaky lies as if it's the most important thing in the world. I can't *not* listen. Plus, the women here don't have new dresses.

I'm surprised when he says, "Amen." It all went so fast.

We close the worship service by singing Psalm 73. Another favorite!

After the service, members of the church surround Father and Mother and Uncle Ed, eager to talk.

Betsie and I slip into an open courtyard. It's a fine, clear evening, but still a little sad. If we were at our own church, we'd be surrounded by friends.

Betsie asks if I saw the other girl in church.

"The one with the curls?" I ask.

"Right. Here she comes."

The girl approaches us, her curls bouncing as she walks. "Hello. I'm Annika."

I don't really want to make new friends. I just want my real friends.

Her eyes shine as she squeezes my hand, then Betsie's. "I'm so happy you could join us."

I want to dislike her, if only for those curls. But it's hard to dislike someone who is so obviously happy to see us.

As usual, Betsie is the polite one. "It's nice to meet you," she says. "I'm Betsie. This is Tess."

Annika smiles. "It's good to have new girls in church."

"How long have you been going here?" Betsie asks.

"This is our third week. Rev. Hoek just graduated from seminary. He agreed to help us even though we're small."

I look around at the dozen or so families. "You *are* small."

33

"We're getting bigger though. The first week we only had seven families. Today we have twice that many." She looks at me. "I hope you come again next week."

"Um, me too." It isn't true, but I don't want to be rude.

I can see Father, Mother, and Uncle Ed. They're still talking with church members. I tell Annika, "We saw a beautiful church on our way into town."

"That's our old church."

"Why did you leave?"

"The minister said Jesus wasn't really born of a virgin. And he didn't really rise from the dead."

I look at her, stunned. "He said that?"

"Well, he said it doesn't matter if those things are true or not. It's the idea of them that matters."

"The *idea* of them?" Betsie wrinkles her forehead. "That doesn't even make sense."

"I know, but our teacher said the same thing."

I agree with Betsie, but I'd still like another look at the church. I ask Annika, "Can we go see it? Can you show us your old church?"

She looks nervous. "I guess. From a distance."

We walk around the corner and down the street. The church is so pretty, with fancy brickwork around the windows and flowers all around. A crowd of churchgoers stands outside.

Annika stops. "This is close enough."

A family leaves the church and approaches us on the other side of the lane.

Annika touches my sleeve. "We should go."

She urges me away, but I hesitate, eager to get a better look. The man wears a black silk suit with a matching hat, very stylish. The woman wears a shimmering green dress with golden ribbons. Her hair is plaited, with tiny circlets peeking out from a pure white bonnet. Their daughter is dressed much the same.

I wave to the girl, who looks to be my age.

"Don't," Annika whispers.

The girl doesn't smile back. In fact, she scowls at me. Like Mrs. Borgman.

The boy, no older than ten, shouts, "Go home, pigs!"

I stare at him, shocked. I turn to his parents, expecting them to issue a sharp rebuke. They say nothing.

"Ignore them," Annika whispers.

I'm sorry, but I can't ignore people insulting me in the middle of the street.

The family moves on, but the boy turns back. "Scolds!"

What does it mean? I want to run away, to keep running all the way home.

By the time we get back to Annika's church, Father and Mother are ready to go. We climb into the wagon and Samson steps out into the lane.

We turn the corner and pass the big state church again. Members still mingle outside. Father nods to them in a friendly way. Mother faces forward and keeps her eyes on the lane.

I sink down out of sight but can't resist a quick look. They're watching us. They don't shout. They don't call us names. But they want to.

Samson trots down the lane to the edge of town and into the countryside. The sun is lower now, casting a golden light across the fields.

Suddenly, Theo sits up. "Look."

At the crest of a rolling hillside stand several magnificent horses, silhouetted against the sky.

"They're huge," Theo says. "Belgians, I bet."

Mother admires the big horses. "Beautiful."

Father agrees. "So regal and statuesque."

Luc says, "What's statue ecks?"

I slump down in the back of the wagon. Wittemeer may have nice horses, but their people are horrid.

CHAPTER SIX

Wednesday morning, I wake early. Market day! And not just any market day. Today I'm going to give Lizbet to Julia for her mother's soon-to-be baby. I wrap her in colored paper and secure the paper with ribbon.

After a quick breakfast, I tuck her under my arm and hurry outside. Theo is already waiting. Father joins us and pushes off from shore. Water gurgles against the sides of the canalboat. Insects buzz and a gentle breeze brings the scent of meadow grass.

Theo cracks his knuckles. "What's in the package?"

I draw Lizbet out of his reach. "Something precious."

"Gold?"

"Ha!" I give him a look of contempt. "I said *precious*. The most precious thing in the whole world."

"A Bible?"

I hadn't thought of that. "The most precious *living* thing."

He scratches his head. "You've got a puppy in there?"

"Not a puppy. A *baby*."

"Oh, right." Mystery solved, he returns to his knuckles.

Father doesn't comment on our conversation. Actually, he's been quiet all morning. I ask him what's wrong. He presses his lips together. "Nothing. I'm sure everything will be fine."

In town, we glide up to the grassy bank of the canal. Father and

Theo set up our booth. I set red and yellow ribbons rustling in the breeze.

Other farmers move about the square, preparing for the day. Father sniffs the air. "I hope it doesn't rain."

Betsie joins me. "Wasn't going to Wittemeer fun? We got home late. What's in the paper?"

"A present for the Jonkeers' new baby. Where are the other girls?"

"I don't know. I saw Nellie, but she said her mother won't let her visit this morning."

The tower clock chimes nine o'clock and Betsie hurries off to her booth. I turn toward mine but stop when I see Julia across the square. "Julia!"

She stops, looks my way, then continues on.

"Julia! Over here!"

She hesitates, then angles over toward me. "I'm sorry. I'm not supposed to talk to you."

"What? Why?"

"I'm just not." She starts to turn away.

"Wait." I hold out my package. "It's a present for your mother's baby."

Her face brightens. She takes the package, fingering the paper. "Oh, Tess. Can I open it?"

"Not until she's born."

"Can I peek?"

I fold back the paper so she can see.

"Oh, she's beautiful." She strokes Lizbet with her finger. "I love her hair."

"It's yarn."

"And I love her dress. Blue gingham is my favorite. Does she have a name?"

"I call her Lizbet, but you can change that if you don't like it."

"No, I love Lizbet. It's perfect."

Julia throws her arms around my neck. "Thank you so much." When she pulls away, her eyes are shining. "I have to go." She turns and races away across the square.

Strange. But Mrs. Jonkeer can be demanding. Everyone says so. She can hardly keep a maid. They quit on her all the time.

I hurry back to my booth. Theo is waiting for me. "You're late."

It's true, I know. But there are no customers yet. I ask him, "Where's Father?"

He shrugs. "One of Mr. Borgman's men showed up. Told him Mr. Borgman wants to meet with him."

"During the market? Isn't that rude?"

"Of course it is. But that's what he said, so Father went with him."

Women are beginning to fill the square, so I turn my attention to them. But several minutes pass, and no one approaches our booth.

What's wrong? I check our display and rearrange some items. Still no customers. I try to catch the eyes of the women as they pass. They look the other way.

Nellie's mother, Mrs. Vogel, comes close, but when I greet her, she turns and moves away. Like I'm a leper.

What's wrong with everybody? I smile brightly, but the passing women ignore me.

Mrs. Veldman examines a wheel of cheese from a few steps away. She smiles a quick, nervous smile, her eyes darting about like a scared doe.

"Good morning," I say. "Would you like some cheese?"

Mr. Jonkeer walks past, eyeing her with a scowl.

Mrs. Veldman shakes her head. "No, thank you." She turns and hurries away.

A shadow falls over the square as clouds roll in from the west. Mr. Jonkeer watches our booth with a look of smug satisfaction.

I lower my eyes. I don't know why. That's just how it is. Rich town folk hold their heads high and say whatever they want. Farmers and other workers doff their caps and keep their heads down.

Mr. Jonkeer moves on, but not far. He strikes up a conversation with Mr. Dekker, the leather man, but keeps one eye on our booth.

The morning passes, and I don't sell a single item. No one even looks at me. It's like I'm invisible.

Finally, the widow Wolters shuffles over. "Business is slow today."

What is that in her eyes? Sympathy? Or humor?

A smile flickers over her lips. "Did you poison someone?"

I want to slap her. Is it wrong to slap a widow? Always? I bite my lip and remain silent.

She chuckles. "You're right to guard your tongue. But I know."

What a thing to say. What does she know?

"I'm just a poor widow," she says, "but I have interests beyond the borders of this town." She lowers her voice. "Even in Wittemeer."

A chill runs through me. Is that what this is about? Because we went to church in Wittemeer?

She points her cane at me. "And now they mean to punish you."

Things begin to make sense—Julia, Mr. Jonkeer, regular customers who won't even look at me.

And yet the widow is here. I ask her, "What about you?"

She picks up a wheel of cheese, turning it over in her hand. "Under the circumstances, I imagine the price is reduced."

I don't even try to hide my anger. "I haven't sold anything all morning, and you want to haggle over the price?"

Again, that smile. "I have so few pleasures left."

I'd like to snatch the cheese out of her hand and whack her with it. But no. At least she's willing to talk to me.

She sets down the cheese and presses a coin into my hand. "Nothing today, but come by my home tomorrow. Bring some cheese. Only your best."

"I can't." I try to give her money back. "I don't even know where you live."

She withdraws her hand and turns away. "Your parents do."

"I...but..."

She shuffles away.

A moment later, Betsie appears at my booth. "Something's wrong. No one will buy our cabbage."

"It's the same here. They look at me like I'm a criminal."

"My father says it's because we went to church in Wittemeer." She's on the verge of tears. "He's already packing up our booth."

I turn to Theo. "Where's Father?"

"I told you. He's meeting with Mr. Borgman."

"I know. But where?"

He starts to tell me I can't interrupt their meeting, then changes his mind. "It's over in the business district. By the bank."

"Show me."

"I can't. Someone has to watch our booth."

"What does it matter? No one will buy from us anyway."

He presses his lips together like Father does when he's trying to make up his mind. "Alright. Follow me." He leads me across the square and toward the town center.

It's not a part of town I visit very often. I'm glad he agreed to come along. He slows down as we approach a narrow courtyard, closed in by buildings on three sides. The open side is strung with grapevines.

As we approach the vines, I hear voices from the other side.

Theo puts a finger to his lips.

I press into the vines far enough to see. Mr. Borgman is berating Father. "I want more production. More profit. Do you understand? More!"

Father says, "We've increased production every year, but we've already made all the easy improvements."

"Then it's time to make the difficult ones, don't you think?"

"Yes, sir. But that will increase costs, and we won't see a result until next year."

Mr. Borgman pounds his fist on the table. "If I wanted your opinion, I'd ask for it. I want increased profits, and I want them now. If you can't manage that, I'll make it up in other ways. Are we clear?" There's a threat in his tone.

He pauses to puff on his pipe. It's a silly gold-mounted long-necked affair, rather than the simple clay pipe of an honest farmer.

"I said, are we clear!"

Father nods that he understands.

Mr. Borgman narrows his eyes. "And now I hear you're rubbing shoulders with those filthy scolds."

Father doesn't respond.

Mr. Borgman spits. "I don't care. I really don't. Just don't let church matters impact production."

"They won't, sir."

"Don't put *your* faith ahead of *my* finances."

"You needn't be concerned."

"I am concerned. I'm *very* concerned." He rises from the table and stalks off into one of the buildings.

Father remains at the table. He rests his head in his hands.

Theo pulls me out of the vines. "Go back to the booth and wait for us."

"Alright." I'm grateful to get away. I don't like to see Father that way.

Back at our booth, nothing has changed. Still no customers. Clouds roll in from the west, darker than before. I cover the cheese as best I can.

At noon, I make my way to the church steps, where the men are gathering to talk. I can't find my friends, so I wait under the old sycamore and listen in.

They talk of the usual things, crops and weather, and how new government policies might affect them.

Mr. Everhart appears with Mr. Jonkeer in tow and makes his way to his perch on the top step. "Another successful market day."

"Yes, yes," a few people say.

Mr. Everhart glances at the lowering clouds. "Looks like rain, but I ordered it to hold off until the money was made." He and Mr. Jonkeer chuckle at his joke.

Others laugh politely.

Father arrives from the direction of Mr. Borgman's office. Uncle Ed is with him.

Mr. Jonkeer notes their arrival and turns to face them. "Theodore, Edward, I didn't see you in church Sunday evening." His voice takes on an edge. "Where were you?"

Father answers, "We attended church over in Wittemeer."

"Why Wittemeer?"

"They have a new minister. We wanted to hear him preach."

"And?"

"He's a fine young man. A gifted preacher."

Some of the men relax, content with Father's explanation, but not Mr. Jonkeer. "I hadn't heard of a new minister in Wittemeer." He turns to one of the other men. "Simon, wasn't the minister in Wittemeer your wife's cousin or something?"

"That's right," the man says. "But they don't have a new minister. He's still there."

"Still there!" Mr. Jonkeer's eyes glitter. "A mystery!"

The one named Simon flushes with importance. He stumbles over himself to share what he knows. "My Catherine spoke with him just this week. He's...or rather...the state church has lost a number of families in recent weeks. To one of those *free* churches."

"Ah." Mr. Jonkeer turns to Father, a sneer on his face. "Tell me you haven't gone over to that sorry lot."

Father faces Mr. Jonkeer. "It's one of the new Reformed churches."

A murmur rises from the men.

"Theodore," Mr. Jonkeer says, "That's beneath you."

"It's a good church."

"What, then?" snarls Mr. Jonkeer. "Are we not good enough?"

Father presses his lips together.

Before he can speak, Uncle Ed jumps in. "The state church has its government support and the government regulations that go with it. In Wittemeer, they're free to worship according to the Bible and the Reformed confessions."

Mr. Everhart snorts. "Are we not free?"

"I'll tell you what freedom we have," Mr. Jonkeer says. "Freedom from old ways of thinking. This isn't the seventeenth century."

Several men laugh.

Mr. Everhart raises a hand, drawing everyone's attention. "The authorities in Wittemeer may tolerate these new churches, but we will not."

A breeze sweeps the square and large drops of rain splatter on the men's hats and shoulders. The heavens open up, and everyone heads for cover.

I hurry back toward our booth but stop halfway there. Through the rain, I spot a patch of color on the ground, a bit of cloth half-buried in mud. It's darkened by rain and mud spattered, but familiar. It's blue. Blue gingham.

Maybe I'm wrong. I hope so. But no, I'm not wrong. It's a ragdoll. My beautiful Lizbet. She lies face down in the mud, with raindrops spattering her back.

I pick her up. Her beautiful yellow hair is matted and muddy. Her face is smeared with mud. I hold her close. "I'm so sorry."

Back at the boat, Theo has already packed the cheese away and carefully covered everything with a tarp. He stands shivering under an awning.

I ask him, "Did you hear the men talking?"

"Yeah."

"Well?"

"Well, what? You knew something like this would happen."

I glare at him. I most certainly did *not* know something like this would happen. "Where's Father?"

"He's not back yet."

I turn and walk out into the rain.

"Where are you going?"

"Home." I start running. I don't care that I'll get soaked. I run when I'm upset. I run when I'm happy too, but now I'm upset. I sneak a peek at Lizbet's filthy hair. Julia would never do such a thing. She's my friend.

CHAPTER SEVEN

When I reach home, Mother takes one look at me and asks, "What's the matter?"

"Everything!" I tell her what happened at the market. "All because we went to church in Wittemeer! It's Uncle Ed's fault."

She hugs me, even though I'm sopping wet. "It'll be alright."

"But what if we can't sell cheese at the market?"

"It'll be alright. I'm sure things will settle down in a week or two."

"My friends won't even to talk to me."

She squeezes me tight. "It'll be alright."

I don't see how.

In my room, I change into dry clothes. Lizbet's beautiful yellow hair lies dark against her forehead. I carefully clean and dry her hair, her face, her dress.

When Theo arrives home, he comes to my room. His clothes are completely soaked. He says, "Thanks for all the help."

"Sorry. What can I do?"

"Nothing. Are you alright?"

"I'm fine." I shift my blankets, so he won't see Lizbet. "Where's Father?"

"Still in town. He sent me on ahead."

"Why would they be so mean?"

He shrugs. Typical Theo. So comforting.

"Mrs. Veldman wanted to buy some cheese, but she didn't dare. Because Mr. Jonkeer was watching."

Theo nods. "Everyone is afraid."

"What will we do?"

"I don't know. Father will figure it out."

"You're dripping. You should change your clothes."

"Not yet. I have to see to the animals."

At suppertime Father still hasn't returned. We eat a silent, somber meal. Outside, the rain still falls.

It's nearly bedtime when Father returns. He walked all the way home. He's soaked through, but he doesn't come inside immediately. He stands on the porch for a long time, talking with Mother.

I watch them from the window. What are they saying? I'd listen in, but that would be rude. And the rain makes it impossible to hear.

I put Luc to bed and go to my room.

Later, Father knocks on my door. "Tess?"

"Just a moment." My room is such a mess. I push everything I can under my bed and open the door. "What?"

He doesn't seem to notice the clutter. "Mother tells me you're upset."

"Yes, I'm upset. No one would buy our cheese. Because we went to church in Wittemeer. Can't we apologize? Won't that make it better?"

"We can't apologize." He pauses. "We aren't sorry."

"We aren't?"

"Uncle Ed was right. We have to worship where the Bible is preached. Even if that means opposition. Do you remember those verses he read last week, how Paul was persecuted?"

"I remember. Luc kept interrupting him."

He chuckles. "Yes, he did. But the point Uncle Ed was making is that we will have troubles in this world."

"But that was in Bible times, not today."

"It's still true." He sits down beside me. "Now tell me what happened at the market."

I tell him. Everything except Lizbet.

He sighs. "I shouldn't have left you and Theo at the market alone. I won't put you in that position again."

"But what can we do?"

"Continue on, trust God."

"But people won't buy our cheese. What will happen if we don't have enough money?"

He puts a hand on my shoulder. "I still have my work with Mr. Borgman. We'll be alright."

He's trying to comfort me, but I don't want comfort. I want answers. "How will we pay for things without the money from Mother's cheese?"

He sighs. "God only knows."

"Of course *God* knows. How will *we* know?"

"We'll have to wait and see."

I hate to wait. He knows that. It's one of my worst faults.

He says, "When I was a boy, did I know I would meet your mother? That we would have Theo and you and Luc? God knew. He only showed me a little bit at a time."

I don't understand how he can be so calm about this. I lay back on my pillow. "Will Theo have a wife some day?"

"I pray he will."

"And Luc?"

He laughs. "Let's hope the poor girl likes answering questions."

I laugh too. It's good to know we can still laugh.

Thursday morning, the rains have passed. Sunlight sifts through thin clouds, turning everything soft and hazy. I go about my chores but can't stop thinking about yesterday—Mr. Jonkeer driving my customers away, angry men arguing with Father, the widow Wolters with her odd little smile.

Suddenly, I remember. I promised to bring her some cheese.

Father is still in the barn, tending to the animals. I show him the coin the widow gave me and tell him what she said, how she wants me to bring her a selection of cheese.

"And you agreed to that?"

"I didn't want to say no. She was the only one who would even talk to me."

"That was good thinking. You better go see her this morning."

"Do I have to? Couldn't *you* do it?"

"I have to work. And she'll be expecting you."

"But she's so...she says such odd things."

He chuckles. "That she does. Shall I send Theo with you?"

Normally, I would hate that. But the widow makes me nervous, so I agree.

Father writes down directions to the widow's apartment. She lives in a long row house called the *Brugplatz*, near the High Street.

He talks to Theo while I fill a burlap sack with cheese.

Soon Theo appears at my side, a scowl on his face. "Why did you agree to go to her house?"

"I don't know. I wish I hadn't."

"Why do I have to go along?"

"It was Father's idea."

"I don't have time for this. I'm needed in the fields."

Father overhears him and says, "The fields can wait. Help your sister."

Theo mutters to himself and stomps off.

I follow him. "Let's get this over with. Then you can get back to the fields."

"Just a minute," he says. "As long as we're going, let's add some sausages." He disappears through the cellar door and returns with a dozen sausages to add to the sack.

Together, we set out for Otten. A breeze ripples over the puddles that remain from yesterday's rain.

In town, Theo turns toward the Brugplatz.

I grab his arm. "Stop!"

"Why?"

That road leads past the market square, the church, and the *Hoofdstraat*, the street where Julia lives—all places I want to avoid. I can't face people today. Especially Julia. "Can't we take a different way?"

He looks at me like I'm out of my right mind. "I'm needed in the fields."

I search for the right words to explain. But he won't understand.

"Whatever," he grumbles, and leads me on the long way around.

The widow's apartment is the narrowest in the Brugplatz, barely wide enough for a door. Her apartment is flanked on either side by much larger apartments.

Theo knocks on the door, waits impatiently, then knocks again. The door opens just wide enough for the widow to peer out. Her eyes narrow when she sees Theo. "What's this about?"

I point to the sack slung over his shoulder. "You asked me to bring you some cheese."

She scowls at me. "And who asked you to bring a clumsy boy?"

Theo sputters to respond, but I interrupt. "It was my father's idea."

She opens her door wider. "Come in, then." It's an order, not an invitation.

We enter a narrow room that ends in a second door, this one painted red. That must lead to her main living area, but she blocks the way. She has no intention of inviting us further in. "It seems you had a little trouble at the market."

I bristle at the half-smile behind her eyes. Theo says, "Everyone is afraid of Mr. Jonkeer."

49

"Ah, Mr. Jonkeer. But people do enjoy your mother's cheese." Her eyes glint with mischief. "Perhaps they'd find their courage if you met them in secret, say, in a back alley."

She directs Theo to spread out the contents of his sack on a small side table, then sorts through the merchandise with a critical eye. She selects three small wheels of cheese. They are expertly chosen, the very best items. "Since no one else wants them," she pauses, "I imagine your price has come down."

"Our price is fair," Theo says. "There's no need to bargain."

"No need to bargain?" She looks at him with disdain. "There's no need for cheese, either, but both happen to please me." She turns to me and gives a little cough. "What can you do for me, child?"

Theo doesn't like being ignored. "If you purchase four small wheels, we can throw in a liver sausage."

"Liver sausage!" She flails about as if she'll faint. "Dr. Brink says it'll be the death of me."

"Half a cheese, then." Theo sounds unsettled now.

She dismisses him with a wave of her hand. "I have no interest in half of anything." She turns to me. "What will it be?"

"If you buy four," I do some quick calculating, "we can throw in another. A full one."

"Better. But really, who needs that much cheese?"

"You can give one to the deacons. For the poor. And it won't cost you anything."

She chuckles. "Now that's thinking." She looks at Theo. "Smart girl, eh?"

"Sure." He rolls his eyes. "She's brilliant."

"One problem, though. I haven't been to church in ten years."

Is she serious? Thinking back, I can't remember seeing her at church.

A sudden clattering noise comes from the back of her apartment, beyond the red door. Then footsteps. The widow's smile disappears.

I step forward. "Is everything alright?"

"Everything is fine." She pays me and scoops up her cheese. "But I don't have time for this today." She guides us back to the door and pushes us out. The door snaps closed behind us.

We stand in the street outside the Brugplatz. I look at Theo. "That was odd."

"*She's* odd," he says.

"Not her. What made those noises?"

"A cat?"

I shake my head. "Bigger. A lion, maybe, or a tiger. Maybe she keeps a collection of exotic animals in there."

He rolls his eyes. "Or maybe she just has a visitor."

"Alright. But why so secretive?"

He shrugs. "Maybe he's a gentleman friend."

"Theo!" I give him a look. "She's an old woman."

CHAPTER EIGHT

Leaving the Brugplatz, Theo and I take the long way back through town. I feel better once we reach the canal. Its waters are swollen with rain, and it glitters in the sunlight. Along the banks, tall reeds bend in the breeze. I suggest we stop and have a picnic lunch of cheese and sausage.

To my surprise, he agrees. He hands me a wedge of cheese and a sausage.

I ask him, "What do you think the widow meant about meeting people in a back alley?"

He bites into a sausage. "Who knows? She's out of her right mind."

I disagree. She's odd, but she always seems to have a purpose behind her words. "I think she means people want to buy from us, but don't want to be *seen* buying from us. Because of Mr. Jonkeer."

"So all we have to do is get rid of Mr. Jonkeer?" He grins. "Does the sweet old widow have any suggestions for how to do it?"

"You know what I mean. We should sell our cheese where Mr. Jonkeer won't see."

"And where is that?"

"We could go from door to door. Like a peddler."

His face lights up. "That might work. We can go to the Veldmans right now. They live right here on the canal. And Mr. Jonkeer won't see." He gets to his feet and marches up the canal toward the Veldmans' home.

Thus ends our picnic lunch.

The Veldmans live in a fine yellow house with green shutters. Theo knocks on the front door and Mrs. Veldman opens it. She wears a light blue apron, dusted with flour. "Hello. What brings you here this morning?"

Theo explains that we have extra cheese and sausage to sell at a good price.

A worried look clouds her eyes. She glances past us, up the lane. "Come in. Quickly."

"We don't mind being outside," Theo says. "It's a beautiful day. We were just..."

I brush past him, grinding his foot with my heel as I pass.

He rubs his foot. "Inside is good too."

Mrs. Veldman snaps the door closed behind us and sweeps us into her kitchen. She selects two wheels of cheese and several sausages for twenty cents. "It's too bad, the way you were treated in town." Then, as if Mr. Jonkeer is still watching, she adds, "Not that I approve of those new churches, you understand."

I ask her, "Shall we come back next week?"

"Yes, yes, please do. But next time, come to the back door."

Theo looks at her, confused. "The back door?"

"We understand," I say. "Next week, the back door."

She leads us through the house to a little door that opens into her garden. She peers through the window, then opens the door and bids us good day.

Back on the lane, Theo grins at me. "That was easy. One house and already twenty cents. If we go to five people today, and five more tomorrow, and five more the next day, we could make..."

He goes silent. Probably struggling to do the math in his head. He may be a big help on the farm, but he's not exactly the head of his class at school.

"Three guilders," I say, "plus what the widow gave us."

"Right. Three." He points to a house set back from the lane. "Let's try there."

"But that's the Harkemas. He's an elder at church."

"So? Elders love cheese. Come on."

"What if they're angry about us going to church in Wittemeer?"

He shrugs. "We won't know if we don't try."

I should refuse, try to convince him this is a bad idea, but I don't. Probably the coins in my pocket cloud my judgment.

Theo leads the way up a tidy flower-lined path and knocks on the door.

Mrs. Harkema appears. As soon as she recognizes us, a scowl settles on her face. "What do you want?"

I tell her, "We missed you at the market. We thought you might like some cheese."

"You thought wrong."

Theo says, "Mother makes the best cheese in the region."

Mrs. Harkema crosses her arms. "I'd sooner go hungry than buy from scolds like you."

I start to back up. But Theo is still praising Mother's cheese.

"Get off my property," Mrs. Harkema says, "or I'll call the constable."

"Come on, Theo." I turn back toward the lane.

He's still talking. "We have sausages too."

Mrs. Harkema slams the door in his face.

Back on the lane, we turn toward home. Theo says, "Don't cry."

"I'm not crying."

"Well...don't."

I'm not even angry at him. I'm upset with myself for letting him talk me into it. Alright, I'm angry at him too.

After a few minutes he says, "Maybe three guilders is too much to expect."

"You think?" I say. "What's five times zero, plus five times zero, plus five times zero?"

He doesn't answer. Probably can't do the math in his head.

At a bend in the lane, he asks, "Who should we try next?"

"No one."

"Come on. One more. How about the Brouwers? This will be our last one."

The Brouwers seem safe enough. They've always been good friends of my parents. Theo knocks on their door. Yes, Mrs. Brouwer is happy to see us and happy to purchase two wheels of cheese.

"See?" Theo says. "How about the Huizens?"

"Alright." At least I know Mrs. Huizen won't yell at us.

She welcomes us in and apologizes for missing us before. "I didn't make it to the market. I wasn't feeling well yesterday morning."

I don't bother to tell her what happened. She'll hear eventually. She purchases a wheel of cheese and several sausages.

I'm ready to go home, but Theo is just getting started. "How about the Bowmans? Gertie is your friend."

It's true. Gertie *is* my friend. And Mrs. Bowman is a friend of Mother. They serve together on a committee at church. Well, they *served* on a committee. I'm not even sure we'll ever go back to that church.

"Come on." Theo marches up to the door and knocks.

Mrs. Bowman opens the door. She's usually friendly, but when she spots us, her frown rivals Mrs. Borgman's worst. "What's this about?"

"We didn't see you yesterday at the market." I try to sound pleasant. "We thought maybe you'd like some cheese."

Her eyes narrow. "You're too good to worship with us but you still want our business?"

Gertie's voice comes from inside the house. "Who is it, Mother?"

"Never mind."

"We have cheese," Theo says.

Gertie appears at her mother's side. "Oh. Hi, Tess."

Mrs. Bowman brushes her back. "Go watch your brother."

"He's sleeping."

"Then watch him sleep."

Gertie gives me an apologetic look and slips back into the house.

Mrs. Bowman glares at me. "You should be ashamed of yourself."

This is a mistake. I turn to go.

"We have sausages," Theo says.

The door snaps closed.

Once again, we turn toward home, walking in silence.

Theo looks at me. "You know who we should try next? The Loomans."

"No, not the Loomans. Not anyone."

"Just one more."

"No." I turn away so he can't see my face. I start running. And keep running. Not because I'm happy.

When Theo gets home, he tries to talk to me, but I stay in my room and refuse to respond. I don't come out until Mother calls us to supper.

At supper, Father asks about the widow Wolters.

Theo says, "She bought several wheels of cheese."

Father is impressed. "That's great."

Theo lays a handful of coins on the table. "And on the way home we sold some to the Veldmans, and the Brouwers, and the Huizens."

He fails to mention the people who called us names and slammed their doors in our faces. He must have forgotten about those.

Father says, "Well done. Maybe you can visit a few neighbors every day. You can—"

I interrupt him. "Mrs. Harkema yelled at us."

He stops. "She yelled at you?"

"It was nothing," Theo says.

"It wasn't *nothing*. And Mrs. Bowman called us shameful."

Father's jaw drops. "She did what?"

"She didn't really—"

"It was horrid!"

"She said what?"

"She didn't."

"She did!"

Mother's voice cuts through the din. "Don't argue at the table."

We all stop in mid-sentence. Father too.

CHAPTER NINE

Sunday morning, Mother comes to my room. "Wake up, Tess. We have to get an early start."

I groan and bury my head in my pillow. "Do we have to go to Wittemeer again?"

"You might enjoy it."

At the breakfast table, I ask Father, "What about our cows?"

He chuckles. "I appreciate your concern for Madam Maas. Mr. Huizen has agreed to stop by and see to the animals."

"This will be fun," Mother says. "Betsie will be there. We'll have a picnic lunch after the morning service."

A picnic with Betsie. That could be fun.

By the time I wash my face and dress for church, Father has hitched Samson to the wagon. I climb in and pull Luc onto my lap.

It's still cool outside. Mother packs our picnic basket and brings quilts for everyone.

Theo emerges from the house, half-dressed and half-awake. He tumbles into the back of the wagon, buries himself in quilts, and goes back to sleep.

Father guides Samson into the lane and turns toward Wittemeer.

Mother glances nervously at each home we pass. Most are still wrapped in darkness. In others a lamp flickers.

Luc falls asleep on my lap. I nod off, too, and don't wake until we're turning off the main road. Morning light angles across the fields.

We arrive in Wittemeer early and sit in the same row we used the previous week. Soon Uncle Ed and Betsie join us.

Gradually, the seats around us fill up. The congregation is still small, but noticeably larger than last week. Annika's family arrives, and she gives me and Betsie a wave.

The elders enter the room, and Rev. Hoek steps behind the pulpit. He opens with prayer, and we sing Psalm 5. One of my favorites! Rev. Hoek reads from Ephesians 4 and Heidelberg Catechism, Lord's Day 4. He talks about the fall of Adam and Eve into sin, and how God's justice requires that sin be punished.

Thinking of God as a judge is a bit uncomfortable. I obey my parents, mostly, and don't fight with Theo as much as I used to, but if God knows my thoughts, then he knows how really wicked I can be.

But Rev. Hoek says we don't need to fear because Jesus died on the cross to save us from our sins. He took our guilt and punishment on himself.

After the service, Betsie and I retreat to a corner of the courtyard. Annika joins us. "I'm so happy you came back."

I do not say, "Me too." But I am happy to see her again.

"Do you think you'll keep coming?" she asks. "Or will you start a new church in Otten?"

"We won't start a new church in Otten," I say. "Mr. Jonkeer and Mr. Everhart won't allow it."

"What do you mean?"

I tell her what happened at the market, how no one would buy our cheese, how no one would even talk to us.

"That's horrid," she says, "but it's the same here. Do you remember that family we met last week? The ones who called us names?"

"How could I forget?"

"Those are the Robertsons. They run the bank."

Betsie starts to giggle.

We look at her. "What's so funny?" Annika asks.

"The *robber's sons*. And they run the *bank*." She starts giggling again.

She does this sometimes. It's embarrassing. I'm afraid Annika will think Betsie's odd, but she bursts out laughing instead.

When order is restored, Annika says, "I have to tell you what Mr. Robertson did this week."

"Yes," Betsie agrees. "You must."

"Back when we went to the state church, Mr. Robertson ordered a carriage from my father. That's what he does for work. He builds carriages. Well, it's finished now, but Mr. Robertson came over to our house and told us he won't pay for it unless we return to his church."

"That's not fair," Betsie says.

"I know. He stood there with his shiny shoes and his fancy hat and made a big speech about how he'd never do business with Father again. Meanwhile, it was pouring rain outside. It was that day it rained so much."

"Wednesday," I remember.

"Right. So, when he finally left, one of the wheels of his old carriage stuck in the mud and broke. He ended up stranded in the middle of the lane."

"It serves him right," Betsie says.

"He hollered at his driver and hollered at his horses, but still the carriage wouldn't budge. So he tried to climb down but slipped and landed knee-deep in mud."

Betsie starts giggling. "I'll bet his shoes weren't so shiny then."

"Father offered to help, but he refused. He put his nose in the air and tried to walk away but stepped right out of one of his shoes."

We all laugh.

"It was stuck fast in the mud. He stood in the middle of the street, trying to balance on one foot. Then he bent over to pick up the shoe and tore a hole in the seat of his pants."

Betsie snort-laughs, which starts me laughing so hard I have to gasp for breath.

"He kind of hop-walked away on one foot, like this." Annika mimics his actions.

We can't stop laughing now, even though people are starting to stare. We're still laughing when Annika's mother appears and tells her it's time for their family to head home.

Annika asks, "Are you staying for the evening service?"

"Yes."

"Oh, good. Then I'll see you tonight." She gives us a quick hug and disappears around the corner.

Betsie and I make our way back to our wagons. She says, "Now we get a picnic lunch. What did you bring?"

"Sausage and cheese and a loaf of bread."

"Mmm." She licks her lips. "We brought ham and vegetables. What did you think of church?"

"It was alright." I don't want to sound too enthusiastic.

"Do you think your family will keep coming?"

"Maybe. I hope not."

She looks disappointed. Then she brightens. "Annika seems nice, don't you think?"

"I guess." I don't want to be disloyal to my real friends.

Theo joins us at the wagon. "Where is everybody? I'm starving."

No surprise there. He's always starving.

"I almost forgot," Betsie says. "We brought pies."

Theo's head turns. "Pies?"

"They have custard inside."

"Well, let's have one."

"They're meant for after dinner."

"I'm hungry now."

"Wait here." She crosses the street to her own wagon and returns with a picnic basket. Inside are seven pies. Each one is the size of my hand. But as she shows them to us, she has second thoughts. "Maybe we should wait."

Theo scoffs at that. "There are seven pies and seven people. What possible difference could it make when we eat them?" He grins, confident his logic is beyond question.

Betsie reaches for a pie, but I stop her. "Don't just give it to him. At least make him do something for it."

"Like what?"

Theo licks his lips.

"If she gives you a pie, you have to tell Father and Mother you don't like this church as well as ours."

He shakes his head. "Can't do it."

"Why not?"

"I like it here. No stuffy rich people looking down on everyone else."

I reach into the basket, pull out a pie, and hold it under his nose. "All you need to do is tell them one thing you don't like about this church."

He wavers. "Alright." He grabs the pie and gulps it down in three bites.

Betsie rearranges the remaining pies. "I probably should have checked with my father first. Maybe that was a mistake."

Theo licks his fingers. "No mistake."

She grins. "Listening to you, that was the mistake." She closes the basket. "Sorry, Tess. No more pies until after dinner."

When our parents join us at the wagon, Father says, "Good news. One of the elders here, a Mr. Meers, invited us to join his family for dinner."

"What about our picnic?" I ask.

"This will be better," Mother assures me. "We'll have a chance to visit with them, find out how things are going here."

I don't even try to hide my disappointment. Dinner with strangers instead of a picnic with Betsie. Better, she says. Better for who?

CHAPTER TEN

We walk to the elder's house, which is down the lane from church. It's a pretty house, gray with reddish shutters. Lace curtains frame the windows.

Father knocks on the door, and who should greet us but Annika!

"Yay!" she says. "I was hoping it was you. Come in."

Mrs. Meers appears at her side and welcomes us into their home. Three young boys crowd behind her. She introduces her family. "Annika is our oldest. She's thirteen." She lines up her boys. "This is Matthew. He's eight, Mark is six, and John is four."

Theo grins. "Where's Luke?"

Luc says, "*I'm* Luc."

The three Meers boys find that hilarious.

Their home is larger than ours and comfortable inside. Two loaves of dark brown bread cool in the windowsill, and the smell of beef stew fills the house.

Mother says, "Everything smells delicious."

"What's 'licious?" Luc asks.

"Tasty," I say.

"What's tasty?"

"Yum," Theo says.

Luc snatches a green bean from the table and pops it into his mouth. "Yum."

Annika's little brothers roar with laughter. "Say it again. Say it again."

Luc is happy to have an audience. "Yum."

The boys start popping beans into their mouths. "Yum. Yum. Yum." Mrs. Meers has to quiet them down.

Soon we all sit down to dinner. I'm hungrier than I realized. The stew is delicious. And the bread. And the potatoes, of course. The cheese is good too, though not as good as Mother's.

Mother glances at Mrs. Meers apologetically. "We left our picnic basket back at our wagon. We should have brought something to share."

Mrs. Meers dismisses that with a wave of her hand. "We have plenty. We were hoping for guests today."

Mr. Meers nods in agreement. "How are things in the church in Otten?"

"Not so good," Father admits. "Our old minister passed away. He was a good man, a good preacher. We miss him."

"And your new minister?"

Before Father can answer, Uncle Ed says, "A wolf."

Father explains, "Rev. Bloem is not one to offend, even when the gospel calls for it."

Uncle Ed repeats his assessment. "A wolf."

Mr. Meers nods. "Unfortunately, I'm familiar with that attitude. Is there interest in forming a free Reformed church, as we've done here?"

"We've discussed it, yes. That's one of the reasons we came here today. We hope to learn from you. How long have you been meeting separately?"

"This is our fourth Sunday together."

"And no opposition from the government?" Mother asks.

"Not directly. They insist we pay for our own building, support our own minister, and provide for our own poor. That's not so bad. We're happy to do it. Our members have committed money and land

and labor. Still, the local assembly has been slow to give us official approval."

I wonder how a church of ten families, or fifteen, or even twenty can afford to support their own minister. And none of them are wealthy.

"What about your neighbors?" Mother asks. "No opposition from them?"

Mrs. Meers glances at her husband. "They don't like that we meet separately."

Mr. Meers butters his bread. "God has been good to us. We never go hungry. But I did lose another customer this week."

Annika winks at me, and I realize he's talking about the robber's son. Betsie claps a hand over her mouth, but still she giggles.

I smother my own laughter but can't stop my shoulders from quivering.

Mother gives me a look. The one that says, "Do we need to get you a doctor, or are you just being extremely rude?"

Mr. Meers doesn't seem to notice. He says, "Several of our members are struggling. People refuse to do business with them. They can't sell their goods and services. Some are thinking of leaving."

"Leaving?" Father asks. He and Uncle Ed both look concerned. "Where would they go?"

"America. They don't want to. But they don't see any other choice."

Father lets out a long breath. "I suppose it could come to that for me, but I would have to be down to my last guilder."

After dinner, Annika and Betsie and I clear the table, then go outside to talk. The Meers have a large garden, much like ours, but no pasture and no barn. Instead of fields and groves, they have neighbors on every side.

Annika says, "We should ask Theo to join us."

I shake my head. "No. We shouldn't."

"What's it like, having an older brother?"

What can I tell her? "He's annoying. Ignorant. Rude."

"I doubt that."

I try to change the subject. "It's a shame you don't have any cute boys at church."

She smiles. "Until now."

I twist my face in disgust, and we all laugh.

The sun is hot, but a gentle breeze rustles the trees. We decide to go for a walk. We make our way up one lane and down another. They all look alike to me. I ask Annika about the long-haired boy who sat alone in the back row.

"That's Kohl. He's in my grade at school. He's an orphan, I guess. No one knows his real name. Our old teacher called him *Koeltje* because he comes and goes like the breeze. Now everyone calls him Kohl."

"Did he go to the state church before?"

"Yes. He sat all alone in the back row there too."

"He could be cute."

"Maybe." She laughs. "But he's not the kind of boy parents approve of."

Honestly, that only makes me more curious.

We turn onto another lane. Betsie says, "It must be hard to be the only girl your age in church."

"It was, but now there's three of us. Do you like it here?"

Betsie giggles. "You mean, apart from the lack of suitable boys?"

Annika smiles. "I'd fix that if I could, believe me. But either way, I hope you come back."

To be honest, I don't *want* to like the church in Wittemeer. But I do like Annika. I say, "It's nice here. But we miss our friends."

"Does your old church have lots of girls?"

I don't like to think of it as our *old* church. I say, "There's Julia Jonkeer..." I pause, remembering the last time I saw Julia. That horrid day at the market. Is she still my friend?

Betsie starts to giggle. "Her mother is going to have a baby any day now."

"And Nellie," I say. "And Johannah, and Susannah, and Gertie—she can whistle."

"And Eva." Betsie grins. "Don't forget Eva."

"And Eva. We're all best friends."

"Will you go back to the market this week?" Annika asks.

"No. My father says he won't put us through that again."

Betsie nods. "My father said the same thing."

"What will you do for money?"

"Theo and I sold cheese and sausage to some of our neighbors. We went to their houses like a peddler."

"What a good idea," Annika says. "I knew he was smart."

"It wasn't his idea."

She winks at Betsie. "He's cute. He doesn't *have* to be smart."

I groan. "Can we change the subject?"

Betsie says, "It's good that you brought in some extra money, though."

"I suppose. Father was happy. But it was horrid. People yelled at us. They called us names."

"Why do they do that?" Annika shudders. "It's no wonder people are leaving the Netherlands."

That reminds me of what her father said at dinner. How can I make sure Father never considers something so horrid? I realize the answer. I need to keep selling cheese so we have more than enough money to live on. And selling to our neighbors isn't the problem. Theo is the problem. I turn to Betsie. "Why don't you go with me this week?"

"Me?"

"You can sell cabbage and turnips. We'll only go to nice customers. We'll skip anyone who might be rude."

"What about Theo?"

"He's needed in the fields."

"Or send him here." Annika grins. "I'm sure I can find something he can help me with."

They both find that hilarious.

Betsie says, "I have to ask my father. Which day? Wednesday?"

"Not Wednesday. That's market day."

"Thursday?"

"We'll sell more if we go *before* market day. How about Tuesday?"

"Alright. I'll ask."

At the evening service, Rev. Hoek preaches from Hebrews 11, where Enoch is taken directly to heaven without having to die. It's one of my favorite Bible stories.

After the service, we load back into our wagon. Before Father can direct Samson into the lane, Uncle Ed stops us. He holds out a picnic basket. "I almost forgot. Betsie made pies."

Theo sits up. "Pies?"

Uncle Ed opens the basket. He hands pies to Father, Mother, Theo, and Luc. When he gets to me, he stops. "Oh! I thought we packed enough."

I look at Theo.

His pie is already half-eaten. "Delicious."

"Don't worry," Mother says. "I can share mine with Tess."

"It's alright," I say. "I'm not hungry."

Theo devours the rest of his pie, then proceeds to lick each finger.

Father directs Samson into the lane. He glances over his shoulder. "What did you think of the church service?"

I wait for Theo to tell Father about something he didn't like.

He sits back, eyes closed, a pie-induced grin on his lips.

I kick his shin. Not hard. Just enough to remind him.

He opens his eyes. "What?"

"Father wants to know what you thought of the church service."

"Oh. It was fine."

I kick him again. Harder.

"Oh..." He sits up. "I didn't like...um...I didn't like that it was over so fast. I wanted to hear more about Enoch."

Father chuckles. "I feel the same way. Rev. Hoek's sermons are so full, and yet time just flies."

Theo folds his arms and smiles. Like he just said something profound.

CHAPTER ELEVEN

Monday afternoon, Father asks me, "How do you feel about selling cheese to some of our neighbors again?"

I hide my smile. He must have talked to Uncle Ed. "That sounds alright."

"Are you sure? Last week it didn't go so well."

"I'm sure this week will be better, but...isn't Theo needed in the fields?"

"Uncle Ed thought maybe Betsie could join you this week. She could sell cabbage while you sell cheese. How does that sound?"

"Sure. If you think so." Best to let them think it was their idea.

Tuesday morning, I do my chores, then fill a burlap sack with as much cheese as I can carry.

Theo walks over and watches over my shoulder. Annoying.

"Aren't you needed in the fields?" I ask.

"Yes. But I want to make sure you really plan to sell some cheese."

I hold up the sack. "Satisfied?"

He steps in front of me. "We need the money."

Betsie arrives in the yard before he can lecture me further. She's pulling a cart piled high with cabbage. And she left room for Mother's cheese.

"A cart! What a good idea." I make a face at Theo. Why didn't *he* think of that?

He knows what I'm thinking and turns away. Probably to the fields. He's needed there.

I add my cheese to the back of Betsie's cart, and we turn toward Otten. It's the heart of summer now, and every day is an oven. Heat waves rise from the lane. Trees shimmer and dance in the distance.

Betsie asks, "Where shall we go first?"

"The widow Wolters. This was her idea. And she bought cheese from me and Theo last week."

Betsie's face tightens. "If you think so."

We walk to town, then take the long way around to the Brugplatz.

As we approach the widow's door, Betsie stops. "What's she like?"

"She's nice. Mostly."

"Mostly?"

"Except when she's, well...not."

Betsie glances about nervously. "Maybe this isn't a good idea."

"Of course it is." I select some cheese and march up to the door, hoping I look braver than I feel.

"No. Wait." Betsie chooses some cabbage and hurries to join me.

The widow answers the door and directs us into her narrow entry-way. "I left Theo home," I say. "This is Betsie."

"I know who she is." She turns to Betsie. "Your father is the one stirring up all the church trouble."

Betsie's eyes go wide with alarm. Her face drains of color.

The widow grins. "Don't worry, child. It's all the same to me. Show me what you've brought."

Betsie doesn't move.

"Today," the widow adds.

Still, Betsie stands anchored to the floor.

I move past her and set several wheels of cheese on the table.

The widow looks them over with a discerning eye and selects the three best wheels. At market I would sell them for fifteen cents, but the widow will want a discount, so I ask for twenty instead.

"Bah." She dismisses that with a wave of her hand. "Too much."

Recovering somewhat, Betsie spreads out some cabbage. The widow picks through her offerings, selecting only the best.

Betsie asks for fifteen cents. Not enough.

"Too much," the widow barks.

Betsie looks at me, unsure what to do. "But...that's the price."

The widow sighs. "All business with this one. No sport."

"I don't..." Betsie falters. "I can't sell them for less than—"

"Stop," the widow orders. "Who else is going to buy them? The Everharts?"

Betsie gulps.

"Ten cents," the widow says.

"Alright."

The widow turns back to me. "And fifteen for you." She reaches for her handbag but stops as a heavy *thunk* sounds from inside her apartment.

We all jump.

I remember the noises Theo and I heard last week and gather my cheese to go.

More noises. Then the sound of breaking glass.

The widow stands very still, like she's struggling to maintain her composure. "Stay here." She narrows her eyes at me. "Do not follow." She disappears through the red door, careful to close it behind her.

Betsie looks at me. "What made those noises?"

"A lion, probably. Maybe a tiger."

Scuffling sounds come from the other side of the door, then a cry of pain.

"An injured lion?" I step closer to the inside door.

"Don't."

My mind races. If I disobey the widow, I might lose her as a customer. But someone is hurt.

Betsie says, "We should go."

It's true, we should. I nudge the door open an inch and listen. Someone is sobbing. I put my face to the gap in the doorway but can't make anything out. Then I spot the widow. She's down on the floor on her hands and knees. She's wiping something up with a towel. Something red. Blood.

I can't take my eyes off that towel. What shall I do? I can leave—go home and pretend I didn't see anything. But the widow might need my help. Still uncertain, I inch forward.

Behind me, Betsie backs away. I should have brought Theo today. I should have brought Mother.

The widow spots me. "Well, don't just stand there. Come in and help."

I leave Betsie behind and step through the doorway. "What happened?"

"Cobie's cut her foot."

In a day bed up against the wall lays a girl. She looks to be younger than me, but only by a few years. Her eyes follow me as I enter the room.

"She knocked the vase off the mantel," the widow says. "I don't know why we have a vase in here."

Stooping to the floor, I pick up a scattered bouquet of flowers.

"Careful. Don't cut yourself. There's glass everywhere."

I shake the flowers and bits of glass clink to the floor.

The door creaks open behind me, and Betsie peeks through. "Is everything alright?"

"Not one bit," growls the widow. "I'm a mad dog. Now go home before I bite you." She lunges in Betsie's direction.

Betsie turns and flees.

"Wait!" I cry, but too late. She's gone.

Through a window, I see her emerge onto the street. She doesn't even stop for her cart, just keeps running.

I face the widow. "That was mean."

"Was it?" A hint of a smile plays on her lips.

I should probably go after Betsie, but my curiosity wins out. The girl in the bed has dark eyes and dark curls. I ask her, "Are you alright?"

"Yes. I just lost my balance for a moment." Her voice is soft, but clear. "I knocked the vase off the table and then stepped on the broken glass. I'm sorry to be trouble."

"She's been sick," the widow explains.

I turn my gaze to the widow's apartment, seeing it for the first time. It isn't narrow and drab like I expected. It's spacious and grand, hung with rich draperies in scarlet and gold.

She notes my reaction and chuckles with pleasure. "Now you know my secret."

"Your apartment seems so small from the lane. How is it possible?"

"I own three apartments. Actually, I own the entire row. But I live in these three. I broke down the walls between them to make one large living space."

"Everyone thinks you're poor."

"That's as I intend."

What a schemer! And to think, I gave her a discount on her cheese. While she lives in luxury.

I should be upset, but mostly, I'm curious. I turn back to the girl, but the widow takes my arm and directs me into another room.

"Who is she?" I ask.

"I told you. Her name is Cobie."

"I thought you lived alone."

"If you thought of me at all."

That stings, but it's fair. "Will she be alright?"

"I've wrapped her foot. I'll have Dr. Brink take a look at it."

"But who is she? Why does she live here?"

She narrows her eyes. "I believe it's time for you to leave."

"I...you haven't paid me yet."

"Ha!" That draws a burst of laughter. "Business first. I respect that." She pulls out her handbag and pays me twenty-five cents for the cheese and cabbage. "But we have one more item of business."

"What's that?" I ask.

"You know my secrets. How much will it cost me to keep you quiet?"

I look at her, puzzled.

She says, "I don't want people knowing how I live. And more importantly, no one may know about Cobie." She counts out six ten-guilder notes. "Promise me you'll keep quiet, and these are yours."

Sixty guilders! That's more money than I've ever seen before. Enough to feed my family for months. Enough to keep Father from ever thinking he has to leave the Netherlands.

But I can't accept it. I tell her, "I can keep a secret. You don't have to *pay* me to keep a secret."

"I'm not big on trust. I prefer a business transaction."

"I can't lie to my parents."

"I won't ask you to. If they ask you if I actually live in a large, well-appointed apartment and oh, does a ten-year-old girl named Cobie live with me, you may answer honestly. Otherwise, all I ask is that you keep quiet."

"What about my brother? He was here last week. He heard noises."

"Tell him it was a cat."

"He knows it wasn't a cat. He thinks you have a gentleman friend."

"Ha!" She lets out another blast of laughter. "If only."

"He suspects something, though."

She puts the guilders in my hand. "These are yours, understand? If your friend saw something, or if you feel the need to tell her, you have to split these with her. If your brother figures it out, or if you feel the need to tell him, you have to split these with him."

"To buy their silence?"

"Exactly."

"What if they refuse?"

"They won't. Trust me, I have some experience with these things."

I look at the money in my hand. Split three ways, it would be considerably less. "And if they never find out, I get to keep it all myself?"

"Now you're thinking."

"But who is she? Who is Cobie?"

"No more questions." She guides me back to the door. "Out!"

CHAPTER TWELVE

Outside of the Brugplatz, the sun is blazing. Blades of grass that sprung up among the cobblestones lie wilted in the heat.

I already have sixty guilders, plus twenty-five cents for cheese and cabbage. I can go straight home. But why not stop at Mrs. Veldman's house? Last week, she invited me to return. I follow the lane and slip into the garden behind her house.

She welcomes me in and purchases two wheels of cheese, as well as some of Betsie's cabbage. Ten minutes later, I'm back in the lane. With more money. Who next?

I can visit the Brouwers again and the Huizens on my way home, but decide to first stop at the Haans, who live in town. They're members of the state church, but they've always treated me kindly. I make my way to their home.

"Of course," Mrs. Haan says. "Come in." She selects a wheel of cheese and some cabbage. "I'm terribly sorry about the way they treated you at the market. I'm not proud of that."

"Shall I come back each week?"

"Please do. Hendrick is partial to your mother's cheese."

Outside again, the sun is still hot, and I stop at the public well for a drink. Before I can draw any water, someone calls my name. "Tess!"

I turn to see Julia Jonkeer. She's smiling and waving. Like she's happy to see me. "Hi, Tess. How long has it been? It seems like ages."

"Hello," I say, surprised to see her. And surprised she's being so friendly. I haven't seen her since that horrid day at the market. And she was the one who made it horrid.

"How've you been?" she asks. "How's Betsie?" She doesn't wait for an answer. "Oh, you probably haven't heard. My mother had her baby. She's a girl. We named her Marianne."

"Like the princess!" I say.

"Isn't it exciting?"

"Does she have dark hair like you?"

"Lots of it. I think she has my eyes too."

"How's your mother?"

"Tired. She's mostly in bed. She sent another maid away, so I have to do *everything*." She points to the well. "I have to fetch water. Can you imagine?"

I don't have to imagine. I've been fetching water ever since I could carry a bucket.

We sit in the shade at the edge of the well and share a drink of cool, clear water.

"What brings you to town? Are you coming back to church? No, I suppose not. But we do miss you."

I should stay angry, but I can't. She's my friend. I'm so glad I have a chance to talk to her alone. Without Eva hovering nearby.

She brings me up to date on the news from town. I tell her about Wittemeer. We talk about our plans for the rest of the summer and the upcoming school year.

It's nice to talk about normal things. But still, I feel like I have to say something about that day at the market. I ask her, "Does little Marianne like her doll?"

Her face grows pale. "Oh, Tess."

I wait, my heart racing.

"I'm so sorry." Tears show in her eyes. "My father was upset, because of the church thing. He took her away from me. He threw her on the ground."

"It's alright."

She buries her face in my shoulder. "He kicked dirt on her, Tess. It was horrid. I tried to explain, but he said I wasn't to speak of it again."

"It's alright."

"It isn't, though. It really isn't."

Three boys enter the square, kicking a leather ball between them. They're older, Theo's age.

"Xander Bloem." Julia grins. "I bet he comes over to talk to you."

I shake my head. "Not after what happened at the market."

But she's right. Xander stops when he sees me and walks over. "Hi, Tess. What are you doing in town?"

I'm not sure how to answer. "Just running errands for my father."

"What's in the cart?"

"Nothing."

His eyes linger on the cart. When he finally looks up, he says, "I heard what happened last week, the way people treated you. I hope you know my father didn't tell them to do that."

It's nice of him to say. I wish I could believe it.

"It sure is hot," he says. "You want a drink?"

I start to tell him we just drank, but Julia elbows me. "Tess was just saying how thirsty she is."

He raises a bucket from the well, fills a dipper, and hands it to me. I take a long drink. "Thank you."

He offers the dipper to Julia, but she refuses. "I'm not thirsty."

He takes a long drink directly from the bucket, then empties the rest of it over his head. Water splashes over his yellow curls, dripping down onto his shoulders. He raises his face to the sun like a wet puppy.

When he opens his eyes again, they find mine. "How's that church over in Wittemeer?"

The question startles me. Does he really want to know? Or is he just looking for information he can pass on to his father? I say, "Fine."

"Just *fine*?" His eyes hold a glint of mischief.

"Better than fine. Fantastic."

He grins. "What's it like? How's it different?"

"It's more...about God, I guess. About the Bible."

"So that's what you want, right?"

I don't respond. Is he mocking me?

Julia says, "My father says your church is more about God and the Bible, but our church is more about being good people and loving our neighbor. Do you think that's right?"

"No, I don't think that's it," I say slowly. "We love our neighbors too." But what *is* the difference? I wish I had the words.

"Do you *want* to go to church in Wittemeer?" Xander asks. "Or is it just your parents?"

"Yeah," Julia says. "I was wondering that too."

I feel trapped. I can say it's just my parents. They'll accept that. It isn't like they can choose to go to church wherever they want either. But I feel I should say more. "I...I like that it's about the Bible. The Bible teaches us *how* to be good people, *how* to love our neighbor."

Xander runs his fingers through his hair. Sunlight glistens on each curl. "It's just sad, though. We miss you, I mean, you know, people miss...your parents."

Julia laughs. "*People* miss her *parents*?"

Xander gives me a sheepish look. "Well...you know."

Julia laughs again. "How about Theo? Do people miss Theo?"

He grins. "Sure. And her other brother. The little guy. With all the questions."

"Luc."

"Right. Luc. People love him. You know what? I'm supposed to be...somewhere else."

Now I laugh. "Goodbye, Xander."

"Bye, Tess. Take care." He rejoins his friends and disappears across the square.

I watch him go.

Julia stands up. "Well, I'd better get going, but I'm glad we ran into each other."

"Me too. I wish the other girls were here."

She grabs my hand. "What a good idea! Will you be here next week?"

"I can be."

"Good. Bring Betsie. I'll bring everyone else. We'll meet here next Tuesday, right at noon."

We hug and part ways.

Overhead, the sun shines in a perfectly blue sky. Birds sing in the trees. I feel like singing too. Julia is my friend again. And next week I'll see all my friends.

Mother is waiting for me at home. "How did it go?"

"Pretty well," I say. I separate out the coins that have to go to Betsie for her cabbage and give the rest to Mother. "The widow Wolters bought some again. So did the Veldmans and Mrs. Haan from town. And I stopped at a few more on the way home. The Brouwers and the Huizens."

"Well done," she says.

I don't show her the sixty guilders. That would only raise questions. And I can't tell her about Cobie. I realize, now, why the widow gave me so much. To control what I say and do. And it's working.

Back in my room, I stuff the guilder notes into a burlap sack. But where can I hide it? I look around at the mess. I could stuff the sack under my bed, but Mother might decide to clean my room one day and find it. I can't risk that.

I remember my old hiding place, where I kept the ring that Hermie

Boven gave me when I was ten. Later, when I found out he gave Eva a silver locket, I threw his ring into the canal. But the hiding place must still be there.

Out in the barn, I climb the ladder into the loft. There it is—a gap where a rafter is notched into a crossbeam. I stuff the sack with the guilders into the gap. It fits perfectly.

When Father comes home, Mother shows him the coins I collected selling cheese. He says, "Thank you, Tess. We appreciate that."

He'll find out eventually, so I tell him, "Betsie went home early."

"Oh?"

"So I didn't sell as much as I hoped."

He squeezes my shoulder. "Every bit helps."

Theo gives me a look, but he can't say anything, not after Father accepted my explanation.

Mother serves split pea soup for supper. One of my favorites. But there isn't much ham to go with it. And only a small loaf of bread.

Father doesn't seem to notice. He leans back in his chair and wipes his mouth with his napkin. "Delicious. Thank you, dear."

Theo gulps down his soup and helps himself to another bowl. Ignorant.

I should give those sixty guilders to Father. They would buy a lot of ham. But they would also raise questions. Questions I can't answer.

After supper, when we're alone, Theo says, "Why did Betsie go home early?"

Anything I say will bring more questions, so I change the subject. "I saw Julia Jonkeer in town."

"Yeah? What did she have to say?"

"Her mother had her baby."

"Oh."

Just that. Not, "Was it a girl or a boy?" Not, "What's her name?"

Not, "Does she look like Julia?" Theo is tragically ignorant about babies.

The important thing is that he doesn't mention the noises we heard in the widow Wolter's apartment last week. He's forgotten already, which means I don't have to split the sixty guilders with him.

At bedtime, when Mother stops by my room, I ask her, "Did you know Julia's mother had her baby?"

"I didn't."

"She had a girl. They named her Marianne."

"Oh, how lovely. After the princess."

"Yes."

"Does she look like Julia?"

"Julia thinks so."

"When did you talk to her?"

"I met her in town today." I hesitate, then add, "Her father says we only care about God and the Bible, and they care more about being good people and loving their neighbor."

"And what do you think?"

"I don't know what to think. Shouldn't we care about *all* those things?"

"We should and we do." She sits down beside me. "Don't let anyone tell you we don't love our neighbor."

"Why would they say that?"

She sighs. "I don't know. Sometimes we see only faults in people we disagree with. But the truth is, it's only by knowing God that we *can* love our neighbor."

"Why don't we go to their church anymore?"

"They do a number of things we don't agree with, but we wouldn't leave the church over small things. The unity of the church is too important."

"So what are the big things?"

"The main reason is that they don't want to talk about sin

anymore. I suppose none of us do. We don't like to admit we need saving. But we need to tell the truth about sin. Adam and Eve sinned against God. We sin too. By nature, we're selfish and proud."

"But they still want to do what's right."

"Yes, but they want to decide for themselves what's right. That's what Adam and Eve did in the garden. That's what Israel did in the times of the judges. They did what was right in their own eyes. We can be like that too. Not what God says. Not what the Bible says. What *we* want."

"So we can't do anything good?"

"Not in our own strength. We end up calling good, evil and evil, good. And the longer we ignore God's word, the worse it gets. I can picture a day when men will decide it's alright to abandon their wives. Go marry someone younger and prettier. Women will reject their own children. And the church will approve."

Is she serious? It's hard to believe.

"But God is gracious." She squeezes my hand. "Through faith in Jesus, we are given a new heart. So we can love him and love our neighbors too."

She moves to put out my lamp, but I stop her. "What do you know about the widow Wolters?"

"Not so much. I know she's had a difficult life."

"Because she's a widow?"

"Yes, and other things."

"Like what?"

"Her husband was quite wealthy. They had a beautiful home and nice things. She rather enjoyed her wealth. But when he died, she was left with very little. I'm sure that's difficult."

"What happened to her money?"

"Why so many questions?"

"No reason."

"It's late." She puts out my lamp. "Get some sleep."

I say my prayers, but I can't fall asleep. I keep thinking about Julia. It was good to talk with her again. Will I ever get to hold baby Marianne? Will she have dark curls like Julia? I wish I had dark curls like Julia.

And Cobie. Who is she? And why does she live with the widow Wolters?

CHAPTER THIRTEEN

Sunday morning, I wake to the smell of Mother's famous almond cake. Am I dreaming? Our supply of sugar is running low. Each day, potatoes make up a larger portion of our meals. And now we're making dessert?

In the kitchen, the cake is cooling on the counter. Theo hovers nearby.

"Don't you dare," Mother says. "We've been invited to dine with the Meers, and we won't show up empty-handed again."

Father hitches Samson to the wagon and we set out for Wittemeer. A nearly full moon hangs near the horizon.

The gentle rocking of the wagon soon puts me back to sleep, and I don't wake until we arrive in town. I keep my head down as we pass the big state church. When we turn the corner, the street is lined with wagons and carts and buggies.

"What's this?" Mother says. "Look at all these people."

Mrs. Meers greets us in the street. "Welcome."

"So many visitors," Mother says. "What's happening?"

"Isn't it wonderful? People hear that the gospel is preached here, and they come."

Inside, the seats are nearly filled. The Kosters are here from Otten. The Vissers too. Mr. Meers and other elders scramble about, bringing in barrels and crates for people to sit on.

We sit two rows behind Annika. She has a quick wave for me. And for Theo, a smile.

An elderly woman walks past, looking for a chair. Theo offers her his seat. It might look like an act of kindness, but he just wants to sit on one of those barrels.

When the seats are all taken, people sit on the floor and even on the steps leading up to the pulpit. Rev. Hoek has to step through them to take his place behind the pulpit.

He opens with prayer, and we sing Psalm 122. One of my favorites! The singing is beautiful. So many voices. People must be able to hear it from blocks away.

Rev. Hoek reads from Isaiah 7 and Heidelberg Catechism Lord's Day 5. He says that because of sin, we don't love God as we should. We don't even love each other as we should. But God still loves us. He sent Jesus to save us. He adopts us to be his children. By faith, we learn to know him as our Father, to love him and love each other too.

After church, Annika and Betsie and I gather at the Meers' home. The house is filled with talk and laughter.

"How big your church is getting!" Mother says. "It's exciting."

Mrs. Meers agrees. "There's such a hunger for the truth."

When dinner is ready, we sit at the table. There is pork and stew, with vegetables and fresh rye bread.

Mr. Meers opens with prayer, and Mrs. Meers thanks Mother for bringing dessert. "That will be a real treat."

Mother smiles. "We're happy to do it."

Mr. Meers passes a basket of bread to Father. "And here's more good news. Rev. Hoek is willing to travel to Otten next Sunday morning to lead you in worship."

Father nearly knocks over his water glass. "Next week already?"

"Can you arrange a place for worship?"

Uncle Ed nods. "We have just the place."

I hold my breath. Not in a barn. With cows.

"Herman Visser's blacksmith shop," Uncle Ed continues. "It isn't large, but it will do."

"We'll need benches and chairs," Father says. "I can help with those."

"Excellent." Mr. Meers refills his glass. "Our church council wants an elder to go along as well, so I'll accompany him."

"With your family?" I ask.

Mother gives me a look. The one that says, "Don't interrupt adult conversation." It's one of my worst faults.

But Mr. Meers isn't angry. "Yes, we all plan to go."

"We'll have you for dinner," Mother offers.

"Thank you." Mrs. Meers smiles. "That will be lovely."

"It's all set then," Mr. Meers says. "Rev. Hoek will lead you in worship in the morning, then return to Wittemeer and lead our evening service."

They go on talking, but my thoughts run ahead. Next Sunday morning, we'll have a church service in Otten. I can invite my friends. How many will come? Julia? Nellie? Eva? Maybe not Eva. But still, it will be like old times. Only better, because Annika will be there too.

After dinner, we all enjoy a slice of Mother's almond cake. I haven't tasted cake in a month. So good!

When the table has been cleared, Annika, Betsie, and I go outside. Annika asks if we were able to sell cheese and cabbage this week.

I glance at Betsie, afraid to embarrass her. But she doesn't seem to mind. She says, "I quit after the first customer. I always thought the widow Wolters was odd. In truth, she's terrifying."

She doesn't mention the fine furnishings in the widow's apartment. Or Cobie. She must not have noticed, which means I don't have to split the sixty guilders with her either.

Instead she tells Annika, "It's Tess's birthday this week."

Annika claps her hands. "How old will you be?"

"Fourteen."

"I wish I'd known. I'd have gotten you a gift."

"You don't have to get me a gift."

"But I want to. I know just the thing. Let's go for a walk."

We agree, but first she enters her house and returns holding three white handkerchiefs.

"What are they for?" Betsie asks.

She only smiles. "It's a surprise." She leads us up one lane and down another until we arrive in front of a squat brick building. "This is our schoolhouse. At least it was. We're trying to start a new Christian school."

Behind the school are rows of blackberry bushes heavy with fruit. Annika hands us each a handkerchief. "Pick as many as you can. It's the only birthday present I can come up with on such short notice."

"It's perfect," I say. "I love blackberries."

The berries are large and ripe and sweet. And there are thousands of them. I eat three for every one that ends up in my handkerchief.

When we've eaten all we can and filled our handkerchiefs, Annika picks a dozen daisies and braids them into a chain. She places them on my head like a crown. "I pronounce you Princess Tess."

"Regent of Schoolyardia." Betsie giggles. "In the land of Blackberrium."

We all laugh. I feel like a princess. Except for my purple fingertips.

We make our way back to the Meers' house. As we sit together in her garden, I tell Annika, "I can't wait until next Sunday. You'll get to meet our friends."

She smiles. "Tell me some more about them."

"You'll love Julia. She has dark eyes and long, dark curls. She—"

"Wait." Betsie interrupts me. "I thought we were angry at Julia."

"Oh. Right. Not anymore. I'll explain later." I turn back to Annika. "You'll love our friends."

"We hope some will come," Betsie adds.

"They'll come," I say. "Some will."

"Maybe."

"Probably."

Annika finishes the berries she took home with her and holds up her handkerchief. It's no longer white. It's stained blood red.

"Murder in Schoolyardia!" Betsie giggles. "I blame the robber's sons."

When we stop laughing, Annika says, "I love these Sunday afternoons together."

I feel the same way. Lilies nod in the breeze. Starlings flit from branch to branch. I ask, "What do you think heaven will be like?"

"Heaven?" They both look at me.

"I think it will be like this. Not *exactly* like this. But Sundays are a picture of heaven, right? And these Sundays are so nice. We went to church together and the singing was beautiful, and we had a good meal together."

"And blackberries," Betsie adds.

I laugh, but I'm serious too. It's good to have friends who can have fun and also talk about important things together.

Theo appears in the yard. Mother sent him to call us to get ready for the evening worship service.

Annika gazes after him. "He's so nice."

"He's not that nice."

"That's alright. He doesn't *have* to be nice."

At church, Rev. Hoek preaches from Hebrews 11:7, where Noah is moved by faith to build an ark. He notes that just as God used the ark to save Noah and his family from the waters, he used the flood to save them from the wickedness that had spread over the earth.

After church, Annika and Betsie join me in our corner of the courtyard. Annika hands me a package.

"What's this?"

"A birthday present."

"But you already—"

"I know. But you need a *real* birthday present. Open it."

I pull back the paper. It's a storybook. A Bible storybook. It's thirty-two pages, with sixteen different Bible stories, each illustrated with a large block print. I don't even know what to say. Books are precious.

"I *love* it," I tell her. "But I can't accept it."

"I've read it a hundred times," she says. "I have the whole thing memorized. Even the pictures. Go ahead, test me."

I open to a page with a picture of a young man and a mighty warrior.

She closes her eyes and recites the story of David and Goliath. Word for word.

I'm still hesitant to accept it, but she insists. "I want you to have it. We're friends now."

It's true.

Mother calls me, and we all hug and say goodbye.

Back at our wagons, I remember to give Betsie the coins I collected selling her cabbage.

"Thank you," she says. "I'm sorry I left in such a hurry."

"It's alright. I think the widow's scary too. Did I tell you I ran into Julia in town?"

"Did she apologize?"

"Sort of. She said it was her father's fault. I believe her. And her mother had her baby. A girl. They named her Marianne."

"Like the princess!" She claps her hands. "I wish I was there."

"That's the best part. You can come this week. Julia's going to tell all our friends. We'll meet them at the well, at noon, after we sell more cheese and cabbage."

Betsie frowns. "I don't think I can make it this week."

"Why not? We can invite them to church at Mr. Visser's blacksmith shop."

"I...I have some errands to run."

She doesn't say, but I think she's still afraid of the widow Wolters. I'm disappointed she won't come, but maybe a little relieved too. If I show up at the Brugplatz with Betsie, the widow will think I told her about Cobie.

We're ready to head home, but Theo hasn't returned to the wagon yet. Father asks me to find him.

I look in the room where we just held church. It's empty. I look in some other, smaller rooms. Nothing. I look in the street. No Theo. Then, in the shadow of a narrow alley, two shapes emerge.

"Theo?"

The shadows part quickly. Theo says, "What do you want?"

"We're leaving. Father sent me to find you."

He turns back to the girl. Yes, a girl. Even in the shadows I can see that. A pretty one too. Way too pretty for Theo.

He says, "See you, Mari."

"Goodbye, Theo. See you next week."

We walk back in silence.

At the wagon, Father guides Samson into the lane, and we make our way home.

Up front, Father and Mother make plans for next week's worship service in Otten. They discuss who to invite.

I know I shouldn't interrupt adult conversation, but I must know. "May I invite my friends too?"

Father glances at Mother, then turns to me. "Who are you thinking of?"

"Julia. And Nellie. And Johannah. And Susannah. And Gertie. And Eva. And..."

Theo rolls his eyes. "And everyone she's ever met."

"No." I glare at him. I didn't mention Cobie.

Father presses his lips together. "I think it would be best, at least this first week, if we only invite people we think might be interested."

"How will we know unless we ask?"

"I plan to invite Johannah's mother," Mother says, "so maybe she'll come. And Nellie's too."

"What about Julia?"

"Not Julia," Father says. "And not Eva."

"You don't want them to go to a good church?"

He sighs. "We already know the Jonkeers and Everharts are opposed to the new churches. That's just asking for trouble."

It's true, I know. But I'm still disappointed. I try again. "Aren't we supposed to tell everyone about Jesus?"

"They already know about Jesus. The truth is, they don't want to hear the gospel anymore. The Bible tells us not to cast our pearls... well, it tells us to use our heads. To be wise. I think that means not inviting the Jonkeers or the Everharts, at least this first week."

I slump back in the quilts. What's the point of having church in Otten if I can't invite my friends?

CHAPTER FOURTEEN

Tuesday morning is hot and humid. I still have Betsie's cart, so I fill it with cheese. My first stop will be the widow Wolters. I hope she'll buy some cheese, but I also want to see Cobie again.

Father sees me filling the cart and says, "Good for you. I'm proud of you."

He must assume Betsie will be joining me, because he doesn't suggest I take Theo. I let him think that.

A few minutes later, Theo walks over. "Where's Betsie?"

Not, "Good for you." Not, "I'm proud of you." Theo can be less than warm and encouraging.

When I don't answer, he says, "Well?"

"She didn't want to come this time."

"Why didn't you say something? Hold on a minute. I'll go with you."

"No."

"Why not?"

"I can do it myself. I have her cart. And you're needed in the fields."

"Last week you hardly sold anything. You can't do that again."

"Or what? We'll go hungry? I'm already hungry." It isn't true, but he's making me angry. "If they won't buy our cheese, then fine, we'll eat it ourselves."

He falls silent. Probably overwhelmed by my logic. But he doesn't walk away. After a moment, he says, "We need to sell it so we can buy other things we need."

"I don't care," I say. "I'm not going to beg for business in Otten. They hate us."

"Don't be so dramatic, Tess. They don't hate us."

"What if they *never* buy our cheese again?"

He doesn't answer.

"Well?"

"Then...maybe we'll go hungry."

I give him my best look of derision. "Who's being dramatic now?"

He ignores that, so I add, "Besides, we'll always have potatoes."

That should silence him. Instead, he takes hold of my hand. "Come with me."

He marches me out past the canal and doesn't stop until we reach the potato field.

"What's your point?" I say. "I've seen potatoes."

"Not like these."

I kneel down, examining the plants at my feet. They should be green and full and ready for harvest by now. But the leaves are pale and dry. They crumble at my touch. "What's wrong?"

"Blight."

A chill runs through me. Last year we lost a third of our potatoes to blight. "How bad is it?"

"It wasn't so bad at first, but with this humid weather, we might lose the entire crop."

I dig into the soil and pull up two small potatoes. They're shriveled and black. And they smell bad. "What will we eat?"

"Exactly."

"What can we do?"

"I'll tell you what some people are doing—"

"Don't." I cut him off. I already know what he's going to say. They're going to America. Like that will solve everything. There has to be another way. And there is. I just have to sell more cheese. Make enough money so we never have to leave our farm.

At the Brugplatz, the widow welcomes me inside. "What did you bring me today?"

I lay a selection of cheese on her little side table.

She examines them carefully, chooses two small wheels, and haggles over the price.

I'm more interested in learning about Cobie than bargaining with the widow, but we need every cent, so I hold out for ten cents.

When the widow's coins are safely in my pocket, I ask, "How is Cobie?"

She freezes, then narrows her eyes like she was hoping I'd forgotten about that.

I haven't forgotten. And I won't move back toward the door until she answers.

At last, she says, "Her foot is improving."

"Can I see her?"

A big sigh. "You might as well. She talks about you day and night."

"Really?"

"She doesn't see many people. You made quite an impression."

She opens the red door and lets me into her living area. I'm struck, again, by the elegant interior of her apartment. Her furniture features carved woodwork. Her lamps have fancy colored glass.

Cobie is in her day bed but sits up when she sees me. "Hello, Tess."

"How's your foot?"

"It hurts. But the doctor says it's healing. Do you know Doctor Brink?"

"I do. When I was two years old, I stuffed a bean so far up my nose he had to come and take it out."

We both laugh.

Even the widow smiles. She says, "When I was a girl, I fell through the ice on the canal. I got so sick, I missed school for two weeks."

Cobie drops her eyes. "I've *never* been to school."

The widow gives her a look. "You know why you can't go to school."

"I'm not allowed to talk to anyone. I mayn't even leave the apartment."

Frustration colors the widow's cheeks. She turns to me. "Our situation isn't ideal. But I teach her what I can. She's learning to read. She knows her sums."

Cobie doesn't say anything, but her eyes hold a sad sort of longing.

The widow's face shows sadness too. "What she needs is a friend, but our circumstances don't allow for that."

"I could come and spend time with her," I say. "When you're busy. Or you need to be away."

She looks doubtful.

"Really. I don't mind. I could stay right now." The words come out before I think them through. What I really need to do is get out and sell more cheese. But I can do that later. Right now, I want to find out more about Cobie.

The widow shakes her head. "I have to go out. I'm supposed to see my brother this morning."

"I'll stay until you get back."

"Can she?" Cobie pleads.

The widow looks hard at me. "Are you sure?"

I look at Cobie. "I'm sure."

"If you don't mind. Just this once." She gathers some papers from the table and takes her cane down from a hook by the door. "I'll be down on the Hoofdstraat. It isn't far."

I know the area. It's where the wealthy people live, with big houses and a leafy park. Julia lives there. Eva too.

The door closes, and Cobie grins at me. "Aunt Ruth told me you might come today."

So the widow has a name. Ruth. And Cobie is her niece. But where are Cobie's parents?

"Where do you live?" Cobie asks.

"In a farmhouse outside of town."

"What's it like?"

"It's nice. We have a barn and a horse named Samson and some cows."

"What's a cow?"

I laugh.

A hurt look comes into her eyes.

I realize, too late, that she isn't trying to be funny. "You've never seen a cow?"

"I'm not allowed to go outside."

"But surely you go into the countryside sometimes."

"Never." There are tears in her eyes.

"Then I'll take you."

She shakes her head. "Aunt Ruth won't allow it. What does a cow look like?"

"They're...um." I can picture Madam Maas, but finding words to describe her is not so easy. "They give milk."

A look of recognition passes over Cobie's face, and she brightens. "I like milk. I didn't know it came from animals. There are so many things I don't know. Can you help me to the window?"

"I'm not sure I should."

"My aunt lets me sit by the window. I won't tell." Her dark eyes glitter, sweet but mischievous.

Minding her injured foot, I help her out of bed. It's harder than I expect. She won't use her sore foot. Instead, she puts most of her weight on me. Together, we inch toward a chair by the window. By the time Cobie slides into it, I'm exhausted.

"Thank you," she says. "I'm sorry to be difficult. Aunt Ruth teaches me things. She reads me stories. My favorite is the one about the little ash girl. Do you know it?"

"I do."

Cobie points to a carriage in the lane. "That's a carriage. Horses pull them and people sit inside. Do you ride in carriages?"

"No."

"Why not?"

"Rich people ride in carriages."

"You're not rich?"

"No."

"Am I?"

I glance around the apartment. "Your aunt is."

She nods. "Aunt Ruth says rich people rule the world, and the only way to not be ruled is to be rich."

From what little I've seen of the world, I can't disagree with her. If my family had more money, we wouldn't have to live in fear of Mr. Borgman. Or a potato blight. Or being forced to leave the Netherlands.

"I've met your aunt," I say. "But who are your parents?"

"I don't know. When I was a baby, my mother had to go away."

"And your father?"

"Aunt Ruth knows, but she won't say. What is school like?"

"We read and write and do arithmetic. And we play with our friends. I like to run races."

"I wish I could go." She knits her brow in frustration. "Are there lots of girls?"

"Dozens. But some are just little. And the older girls ignore us."

Cobie has lots of questions—about my family, about school and those other girls.

I answer as best I can. We talk for almost an hour. Then Cobie stops in mid-sentence. The widow has appeared in the lane, making her way back toward us. Cobie turns to me. "Better help me back to my bed."

I spring to my feet. "Quick. Put your arms around me."

She wraps her arms around my neck.

"Good. Now move your left foot forward."

"Like this?" She shuffles her feet randomly.

"Left," I say. "Other left."

"Oops." She starts giggling. "Which is left again?"

Soon we're both laughing.

She steps on my foot, and I nearly lose my balance.

We make progress, but slowly. My legs ache, and my breath comes in gasps. Finally, we reach the bed. I tilt Cobie onto the mattress as the outside door opens and closes.

Cobie sighs contentedly and sinks back onto her pillow.

I lift her bandaged foot and slide it under the blankets as the inside door opens.

The widow enters the room. Her eyes shift from Cobie, who is grinning, to me—my face flushed with effort. She says, "What's going on here?"

"I...we..." I stumble for a response.

Cobie smiles innocently. "Tess was helping me with left and right."

CHAPTER FIFTEEN

The widow hangs her cane up on a hook by the door and sets some papers on the table.

I ask her, "Did you have a good visit?"

She looks at me, confused.

"With your brother."

"Oh, yes." A hint of a smile shows on her lips. "A productive visit. I got what I wanted. How was Cobie?"

"We had a nice time."

"Good. Come with me." She directs me into another room. "I've raised Cobie from an infant. But she's getting older now. She needs someone closer to her own age."

"She told me she's not allowed to go outside. That's horrid."

The widow's face turns grim. "It's necessary."

"Why?"

"It's a long story, which I have no desire to tell, and you have no need to hear."

"But—"

"But nothing. Thank you for staying with Cobie. Now, I have a business proposal for you."

"A business proposal?"

"I want you to be Cobie's friend."

"Alright."

"I'll pay you."

"You don't have to pay me."

"I *want* to." She reaches for her handbag. "That's what makes it a business proposal."

"I can't accept money to be a friend. I'll come whenever I can."

"I don't want you to come whenever you can." Her face turns hard. "I want you to come when I *tell* you to come."

The whole idea seems odd. "I'll come sit with Cobie whenever you want, but not for money. Stop talking about money."

She shakes a fistful of guilders at me. "I'm a woman with no husband. This is what I have."

I stare at the money. We *do* need money. We *really* need money. But it isn't right. Not to be a friend. "My mother says you used to be wealthy. She thinks you're poor now."

The widow looks away. "We owned half of this town. Then my husband died." She sinks into a chair. "My family thought it best to let my brother handle my finances. God forbid a woman should do it."

"But now you're rich again."

She straightens up. "That's right. Circumstances change. My brother...well, never mind that. Now I care for Cobie, and he allows me to control my own money. Our little business arrangement."

"But you always go to the market in a ragged skirt."

A glint of humor shows in her eyes. "I live better than ninety percent of the people in Otten, and they think I'm barely getting by. It's one of life's little pleasures."

"I still can't take your money. Not to be Cobie's friend."

"You go to church. Surely you understand the concept of a bargain."

I stare at her, confused.

"That's what the church offers, isn't it? You obey their rules—no cursing, no lying, no stealing—and they let you go to heaven when you die."

What a horrid thing to say. "That's not...we don't obey God so *that* he'll save us. We obey him *because* he saved us. It's not like a bargain at all."

"Are you so sure?"

"Yes. It's more like...family."

"Family?"

"God loves us because we're his children. Like you and Cobie. Well, not exactly, but you know what I mean."

"I most certainly do *not* know what you mean."

"You don't love her because..."

"You know *nothing* about us." Her eyes flash with anger, but she quickly douses the flames. "I don't want to argue with you."

I look to the door. "Should I go?"

"Please don't." She raises a finger. "Wait here one moment." She leaves the room and returns with a moist rag. "Wipe down my mantel, please."

I stare at the rag.

She points to a large wooden mantel over her fireplace. It holds a Delft plate, a small painting, and a clock.

The plate isn't heavy, but my hands shake for fear I'll drop it. I wipe the mantel where the plate was and replace it. Next, I pick up the painting.

"Careful," she says. "The plate means nothing to me, but I'm rather fond of my Vermeer."

That's not a name I recognize, but the painting is pretty. I set it off to the side. Then the clock. I wipe down the mantel and carefully replace both items.

"Good." She leads me into another room with another fireplace and another mantel. "Clean this one, please."

I wipe down the mantel and replace the items that were on it.

"Excellent. I want to hire you to help me clean my apartment."

"Alright."

"I'll pay you ten guilders per week."

"Ten guilders?" That's way too much.

"I want you here by nine o'clock every Tuesday and Thursday morning. You'll clean this mantel when you get here and the other one at noon. In between, you'll visit with Cobie."

"Ten guilders to clean two mantels?"

"And sit with Cobie in between. If things work out, maybe you can tutor her. Are you a good student?"

"Yes."

"Then it's settled. Not when you can. Not when it's convenient. Every Tuesday. Every Thursday. Understand?"

"I understand."

"And if anyone asks?"

"I'm helping you clean your tiny apartment."

She chuckles. "That's right."

"I'll have to get my parents' permission."

"They won't object."

Actually, they *might* object. Father will tell me how young I am. He won't like me taking a job in town. But I'll have to convince him. It's a lot of money. Just what we need.

We head back into the main room, and I move toward the door.

The widow stops me. "Do we have an agreement?"

I glance at Cobie, who's watching my every move. I remember what she said earlier about not being allowed to go outside. "I have one condition."

The widow narrows her eyes. "You what?"

"I want to take Cobie outside."

Cobie sits up, eyes wide.

The widow shakes her head. "Impossible."

"She's like a prisoner here. Let me take her outside."

"You don't understand." The widow's voice trembles. "If people find out about her, there will be questions, questions that threaten my ability to control my money. I can't risk that."

Fear shows in her eyes, but I hold my ground. "You don't understand how horrid things are for Cobie. She *needs* to go outside."

"I'm sorry. No."

"Just for an hour."

"No."

"I could do it after dark."

"No."

"There has to be a way."

She shakes her head.

I remember Cobie's tears earlier. "Then we have no arrangement."

"That's absurd." She crosses her arms.

I'm not sure what to do. Should I go? I head toward the door.

"Wait." She holds up her hand. After a long pause, she says, "You may take her outside, but only on one condition. My condition."

"Tell me."

"You won't like it."

"I'll do it."

"It will have to be on a Sunday morning."

"Sunday!" My voice trembles with frustration. "That's the one time I can't do it. You *know* that. I'll be in church."

"Everyone will be in church," she says. "That's why I can allow it. No one will see."

"I can't."

"That's the arrangement. Sunday morning or not at all."

"Can we?" Cobie asks. "Can we really go outside?"

It feels like I'm being pulled apart. I want to be a friend to Cobie. But not on Sunday. Especially this Sunday. Rev. Hoek is coming to Otten. Annika too. And my friends from town will be in church. I look into Cobie's deep dark eyes. "I'm sorry. I can't."

"I promise I'll be good," she pleads.

"I have to go." I start for the door, but the widow stops me. She holds out ten guilders. "These are yours if you accept the terms we discussed. Take them and start Thursday. Or leave them and never come back."

I'll never be able to come on Sunday. I'll never be able to take Cobie outside. But we need those guilders. Avoiding Cobie's eyes, I take the money and go.

CHAPTER SIXTEEN

I step into the street outside the Brugplatz, feeling a bit dazed. Did that just happen? And what should I do now? My friends won't arrive at the well for another hour. I already have ten guilders but still feel the need to sell cheese. If our potato crop fails, we'll need every guilder we can get.

The sky overhead is blue with wisps of white clouds near the horizon as I make my way to the Veldmans' home. It's still difficult for me to walk up to someone's house and try to sell them something, but Mrs. Veldman was happy to see me last week. She invited me to return. When I reach her home, I slip through the garden gate, then knock on the back door.

The door opens, but only an inch. Mrs. Veldman's face appears in the gap. "Go away."

"I have Mother's cheese."

"Leave." She looks frightened. "Don't come back."

"But I..."

"We don't want trouble." The door snaps closed.

I stare at the door. What can this mean? I want to run away, to run all the way home. But I need to sell some cheese. I gather my courage and return to the lane. Clouds are gathering in the west, but the sun is still shining. I decide to visit Mrs. Haan.

"No, thank you." Mrs. Haan's voice sounds firm and practiced. No anger. No name-calling. And no explanation.

"Shall I come back next week?"

"No, thank you." The door closes.

I don't know what to think. Last week, Mrs. Veldman and Mrs. Haan both invited me to return. Now they won't even talk to me.

Suddenly the door opens again and Mrs. Haan says, "I'm sorry, Tess. Please come in."

She sits me down at her kitchen table. "You deserve an explanation. We love your cheese, and we love your family, but...well, Hendrick is just getting established in his business, and we can't afford any trouble. Do you understand?"

I nod, but honestly, I don't understand. I don't want to.

She leads me back to the door. "Take care, Tess. And be sure to visit us again when all this settles down."

Outside again, I wonder, why this sudden change? Someone must have figured out I'm selling cheese to members of the state church.

Someone named Xander Bloem. He saw the cheese in my cart. He must have told his father, who probably informed Mr. Jonkeer. And Mr. Jonkeer forbade people to buy from me.

The clock strikes noon as I arrive at the well. But there is no sign of my friends.

A maid approaches with two buckets. She gives me a weary smile, fills her buckets, and makes her way back down the lane. The square is empty again. Where are my friends?

Two boys appear and approach the well. They drop stones into it, waiting to hear the stones splash, then wander off. Still no friends. My heart sinks. Did they forget about me? Or did they never intend to come?

Finally, girls' voices reach my ear. And Julia's laugh. Five girls enter the square—Julia, Nellie, Johannah, Susannah, and Eva. And to think, I was about to give up on them. Of course they came. They're my friends.

Julia spots me first and races across the square. "Tess!"

We all gather around, sharing hugs and hellos.

"Where's Betsie?" Julia asks.

"She couldn't come. Where's Gertie?"

"She had to watch her little brother." Julia takes my hand. "It's so good to see you again."

Nellie agrees. "We miss you."

Johannah says, "Church isn't the same without you."

Only Eva seems cool. "Will you come back to church next Sunday?"

They all look to me, waiting for my response.

"I...I don't think so," I say.

Eva turns up her nose. "Our teacher says it's wicked to leave the church."

"I still go to church. Just a different one."

"A bad one."

Yes, I want to slap her. But I'm nearly fourteen now. Old enough to control my temper. I want to tell them we're having church at Mr. Visser's blacksmith shop on Sunday morning, but Father warned me not to. I hate not being able to tell them everything.

Suddenly, I remember—Johannah and Nellie might know already. Mother invited their mothers.

I study their faces, but neither gives any indication they know. That makes me worry. Johannah knows how to keep quiet, but Nellie can't keep a secret to save her life.

Julia reaches into her pocket and pulls out a tiny package, wrapped in colorful paper. "I got you a birthday present."

"Really? For me?"

"Open it."

"It isn't my birthday yet."

"Close enough. I won't tell."

I open the package. Inside are two hair pins. They have braided gold stems topped with soft orange tulip blooms.

"Thank you. I love them."

"Aren't they pretty?"

"And orange is my favorite color."

"I know," Julia smiles.

Eva isn't ready to drop the subject from earlier. "What about school?" she asks. "Will you still come to our school?" It feels more like a challenge than a question.

"Of course." I try to sound confident even though Uncle Ed still talks about wanting to start a Christian school. Free of government control.

"Enough about that," Julia says. "Tess, I wish you could see little Marianne. She's such a precious baby."

Nellie says, "She looks just like Julia."

Johannah disagrees. "She has a fat little face."

Eva says, "All babies look alike."

I don't say anything. It's hard to have an opinion about a baby I've never even seen.

They eagerly tell me everything I've missed. Old Mr. Bannister spilled his pipe in church and started a fire. His son had to stomp it out. Mrs. Borgman has a new dress with layers and layers of French lace, which she bought in Paris. Peter, the no-good baker's boy, tried to steal meat at the market, but the butcher's dog caught him and bit him in the leg.

They talk and laugh, but I feel somehow distant. Like they're just talking to each other. Like I'm listening through a window. An outsider with my own friends.

A starling swoops down and sits on a nearby ledge. Its feathers are black as midnight. White flecks twinkle like stars across its belly.

I'm reminded of Sunday, when Betsie and Annika and I talked of lilies and starlings. I ask, "What do you think heaven will be like?"

They stop talking and stare at me.

Eva scrunches up her face. "Let's not talk about church."

Susannah agrees. "It isn't even Sunday."

I try to explain. "That's not what I...it's just...do you think there will be starlings in heaven? And lilies?"

Eva says, "You just want to talk about heaven so you can tell us we're sinners. Don't be such a scold."

I can't even speak. I'm not a scold! I wait for one of the others to tell Eva that.

No one does.

With that one word, Eva has made me invisible. "Scold" means I think I'm perfect and everyone else is horrid. It means they can safely ignore me and anything I say.

Finally, Julia comes to my rescue. Not by saying I'm not a scold. Not by saying Eva is horrid. But by changing the subject. She says, "Let's race. To the schoolyard and back."

Nellie claps her hands. "Yes."

Johannah agrees. Susannah too.

Only Eva refuses. "I have new shoes. They're not meant for running."

"Then we'll run barefoot." Julia kicks off her shoes. "Come on. Tess turns fourteen this week. It's in honor of her birthday."

"I'm *already* fourteen," Eva says. "Nobody ran a race for *my* birthday."

"Better kick off those shoes." Julia grins. "If Tess wins, you have to go to church with her."

Everyone laughs. Everyone but Eva. "Never." She walks away. "If you had shoes like mine, you wouldn't race either." Then, when she's twenty paces off, she jumps out of her shoes and launches across the square toward the schoolhouse.

Not fair! We all kick off our shoes and pursue her.

It's four blocks to the schoolhouse and back. Eva runs with long strides, but ungainly. I know I can catch her. Johannah and Nellie run well but do better in short sprints. Susannah usually comes in last. That leaves Julia.

By the time we reach the business district, Julia and I catch up to Eva. We move to pass her, but she veers toward the buildings, cutting us off.

We drop back and try the other side. She veers to that side, but not quick enough. We both get past.

Julia and I are side by side when we reach the schoolhouse, touch the wall, and turn back.

Eva doesn't bother touching the schoolhouse like she's supposed to. She turns back at the gate, retaking the lead.

Again, not fair. But it doesn't matter. We soon catch her.

Julia and I race side by side through the business district. Ahead of us, Mr. Borgman steps out of the bank, studying a thick ledger book. He's puffing away on his absurd pipe and sweating through his shirt. I'm afraid he'll recognize me and say something, but his eyes are only focused on his profits.

I start to build a lead over Julia. It feels good. Even if I win, Eva will never come to church with me; I know that. But it will be fun to hear the other girls tease her about it.

As we approach the well, footsteps begin to gain on me. Julia. I try to pick up my pace, but my legs just won't.

With fifty paces to go, she passes me. Her stride is compact and efficient. Her long dark curls stream out behind her.

At the well, she pulls up, a grin on her face.

I'm second. Next comes Nellie, Johannah, Eva, and finally Susannah.

"Last again," Susannah pants.

I want to point out that Eva cheated. She didn't touch the school-house wall. But I don't dare say anything. They might think I'm being a scold.

Eva bends over, breathing heavily, then says, "Tess didn't win, so she has to come back to church with us. That was the bet."

The girls all look at me.

I don't know what to say. Is she serious?

Julia laughs like it was a good joke. Then everyone laughs. Everyone but Eva.

The clock strikes one o'clock and Eva says, "I have to go. Mother is ordering some new fabrics today. She said you girls may help choose."

She knows Julia loves to pick out fabrics. And she knows I won't feel welcomed at her house.

"Let's do that later," Julia says. "Now we have Tess."

Eva sighs loudly. "It has to be now."

I can tell some of them want to go. And I don't want to be the reason they miss out on something fun. I say, "I better get back home. I still have chores to do."

Julia looks disappointed. "Alright. But let's do this again next week."

Everyone agrees. Together, they head across the square toward Eva's house.

I watch them go. Alone with my cart of unsold cheese.

CHAPTER SEVENTEEN

After my friends have gone, I sit with my back to the well, admiring my new hair pins. They are truly the prettiest things I've ever owned. Not the most precious. That would be the Bible storybook Annika gave me. But the prettiest.

Eventually, my thoughts return to the ten-guilder note that the widow Wolters gave me. A real job, with real money. But will Father allow me to work in town? I'll have to wait until just the right time to tell him.

I should get up and try to sell more cheese, but the thought of it frightens me. Especially after the way Mrs. Veldman and Mrs. Haan treated me.

A figure approaches the well, a bucket in each hand. Xander Bloem. Looking all happy and sunshiny. He says, "Hi, Tess."

I shove Betsie's cart at him. "It's cheese. But you already know that. Thanks to you, no one will buy from me now."

He rolls the cart aside. "What are you talking about?"

"Don't pretend. You know what you did."

"Wait, what did I do?"

Tears threaten, but I fight them back.

"Are you crying?"

"No."

He gives me his handkerchief.

I throw it on the ground. "Did you tell them to call me names too?"

"Who called you names? What names?"

"The usual ones."

He sits down beside me. "Sorry."

I slide over so there's another inch between us. Is he admitting what he's done? Or just saying he's sorry that people call me names?

"I didn't say anything. Honest." He points at my cart. "You've been pulling that thing all over town. Anyone could have seen you."

It's true. That doesn't mean he didn't do it, but it's true. Right now, I really need to blow my nose. I pick up his handkerchief and use it, then offer it back to him.

He grins. "Keep it. I'm feeling generous."

We sit in silence. Finally, he says, "People call us names too, you know."

"Who? What names?"

"Your people, your ministers, they call us names."

"Like what?"

"I can't even repeat them. Not to a girl. Trust me, they're bad."

At supper, Father asks if Betsie and I sold much cheese and cabbage. I tell him, "There's no use trying to sell cheese to our neighbors anymore. Mr. Jonkeer won't let them buy from us."

"I can take over," Theo says. "I don't mind getting yelled at."

Father shakes his head. "I spoke with Uncle Ed today. He warned me this might happen. He's lost some of his customers too."

"I don't mind," Theo insists. "I get yelled at all the time."

But Father's mind is made up. "We'll find some other way to make money."

"Mr. Jaeger offered me a job," Theo says. "In Amsterdam."

"We don't want you in Amsterdam." Mother adds some beans to Luc's plate. "We should be together. We're a family."

"What about America?" Theo asks. "We could be together there."

Father sighs. "We can't escape trouble in this life. Not by running away. Only at the cross. Besides, as long as I can manage Mr. Borgman's farm, we'll be alright. Times will be tight, but we'll manage."

"What about church? America has freedom of worship."

Father nods. "I won't rule it out. But only as a last resort."

I don't like it when they talk about America. Even as a last resort. Reaching into my pocket, I give Father the money I got from the widow.

He looks at it, shocked. "This is ten guilders."

"It isn't from selling cheese. The widow Wolters wants to hire me."

"Hire you?" Mother looks confused. "To do what?"

"To help clean her apartment."

Theo snorts.

I look at him. "What's so funny?"

"Clearly, she hasn't seen your room."

Father frowns. "You're only thirteen."

"I turn fourteen this week. And we need the money."

Mother still looks confused. "Her apartment is so tiny. Did she say why she needs your help?"

I can't answer without giving away the widow's secrets.

"She *is* getting older," Father says.

Mother shakes her head. "Not *that* old. She's probably just lonely. How long has it been? Twelve years? And no one to talk to."

That seems to sway Father. He turns to me. "I don't mind you visiting with her from time to time."

"She was very specific. She wants me there from nine until noon, every Tuesday and Thursday."

"That's very odd," Mother says.

"*She's* very odd," Theo says.

I point to the note in Father's hand. "We need the money."

He stares at it. "This is too much."

Mother agrees. "I don't think we should accept *any* money from her. She's a widow. It's our Christian duty to help her."

Father nods and puts the note back in my hand. "Tell her you'll be happy to clean her apartment, but we can't take her money."

I want to scream. How can I not? The widow isn't poor! She's rich! But I can't tell anyone.

Later, in my room, I sprawl on my bed. The tragedy!

For half a minute, I just lay there, but then I sit up. The solution is obvious. If my parents knew the truth about the widow, they'd accept the money. Well, I know the truth. I'm going to keep the money.

I don't want to lie. But this isn't lying. Yes, it's misleading. But what else can I do? The widow won't take the money back anyway. I know it seems wrong. But it *isn't* wrong.

Outside, rain clouds are scudding in from the west. I race to the barn and climb up into the loft. I add ten guilders to the sixty I got last week.

The rain begins gently, then starts to pour. I remain in the loft and listen as it pelts down on the roof. I try to imagine what the future might hold. I'll continue to visit Cobie and clean the widow's apartment, earning ten guilders each week. My secret stash of money will continue to grow.

Then one day, Father will sit us down and tell us his farm income isn't enough to pay our bills. Not without Mother's cheese. Not without a healthy potato crop. As a last resort, we have to leave the Netherlands and go to America.

Then, in our darkest hour, I'll lay a stack of guilders on the table and calmly ask, "Will this help?"

He'll throw his arms around me. "Tess. You've saved the day! We can stay in our home and continue to live as we always have."

It might not happen exactly that way, but pretty close.

At bedtime, Mother stops by my room. "Friday is your birthday. Are you getting excited?"

"I am. It's so hard to wait." Even though I know we don't have money for presents this year, or cake, or anything fancy, it's always fun to have a birthday.

She smiles. "I remember *my* fourteenth birthday."

I already know the story, but I always like to hear it again. When Mother turned fourteen, Grandmother first began teaching her the fine art of cheese making. This time Mother ends the story with, "and Friday morning, I'll begin teaching you."

I've known this since I was a girl, but it's exciting that it's finally going to happen.

When we finish making plans for my birthday, she asks about my visit with the widow Wolters.

I quickly skim over that, careful not to tell any secrets, then change the subject. "I saw my friends today, when I was in town. Julia and Eva. Nellie and Johannah and Susannah. We raced to the school-house and back."

"That sounds like fun."

"I came in second place."

She smiles. "You get your speed from your grandmother. She was always light on her feet."

"Did she run races in school?"

"She did. And she won."

"When did people start running races?"

"I think they always have."

"In Bible times?"

"The apostle Paul talks about runners and races in some of his letters."

"What about before? Like Shem, Ham, and Japheth?"

She chuckles. "The Bible doesn't mention it, but I expect they did. Maybe even Adam and Eve."

Thursday morning, I return to the Brugplatz. The widow Wolters lets me in and leads me into her main living area.

Cobie is sitting up in her day bed. "Hi, Tess."

"Hi, Cobie."

The widow shows me where she keeps her cleaning supplies, and I get to work on her first mantel. Just as I finish, there's a knock on the door.

"That'll be the doctor," the widow says. She returns a moment later with Dr. Brink.

He's surprised to see me. He turns to the widow. "Another abandoned child for your collection?"

"Never mind her. Look at Cobie's foot."

Cobie sticks out her foot. He examines it carefully, humming as he works.

The widow grows impatient. "Well?"

He continues his examination. "Have you soaked it as I instructed?"

"We've followed your instructions to the letter."

"It seems to be healing nicely."

She eyes him coolly. "Have *you* followed *my* instructions?"

"Of course."

"To the letter?"

"You know I have. I'm always careful to maintain your privacy. And I appreciate your generous...expressions of gratitude. You always seem to find my preferred variety and vintage. I wish I knew your sources."

"Never mind my sources. Just keep to the bargain and your cellar will never run dry."

I have no idea what they're talking about. Some sort of secret code. But clearly the doctor has agreed to some "business proposal" laid out by the widow in order to keep her secrets hidden. Just like me.

He gives the widow a bottle of ointment to rub on Cobie's foot each night.

She sets the ointment on the table. "I'll have my man pay you a visit in the morning."

"Thank you. Much appreciated. Mrs. Brink thanks you as well. At least she would, if she knew anything about me being here. Which she doesn't."

"As it should be. Good day." With that, she escorts him to the door and out into the street.

When she returns, she sits down at the table with a newspaper. She doesn't have any errands to run today, so she plans to stay in. That makes it difficult for me and Cobie to talk about anything interesting.

Cobie suggests we play a game of chess, which the widow taught her and which I learned in school. She beats me soundly in three straight games.

CHAPTER EIGHTEEN

Today is Friday, July 31. My birthday! But I still have to do my chores. I feed the chickens, gather eggs from the hen house, and weed the beans in record time.

Why so quickly? Because Mother promised to begin teaching me to make cheese today.

But she's in no hurry. She sweeps the front steps and the path to the lane. Then the back steps. Then the front steps again. I play with Luc while she waters the petunias in their window boxes and the roses on the lattice.

At nine o'clock, Mrs. Huizen arrives. "Hello, Tess," she says. "Happy birthday!"

"Thank you."

When Mother isn't looking, she slips me a piece of candy.

I've always liked her. She's a grown woman and married but still remembers what it's like to be a girl.

Luc is happy to see her too. He says, "Why are you here?"

She grins at him. "To keep a certain someone out of mischief."

"What's mischief?"

She picks him up and holds him high over her head. "You are."

Content that Luc is in good hands, Mother leads me to the cheese shed.

In the center of the shed is a cookstove and beside that a stack of wood. Under Mother's careful direction, I start a fire in the stove.

Once it's going, she says, "Now we wait."

"For what?"

"For the stove to give off a steady, consistent heat."

When the fire settles down and the stove is ready, she helps me pour several gallons of fresh milk from Madam Maas and the other cows into a large cooking pot. We place the pot on the stove so the milk can warm.

"Now we wait."

She pulls up a stool and I do the same. I ask her, "Will we keep making cheese even if no one will buy it?"

"Milk doesn't last," she answers. "Cheese does. Hopefully, there will be better days ahead."

"Soon?"

"We can hope."

"I don't want to *hope*," I say. "I want to *know*."

She smiles, but there is uncertainty in her eyes. "We can't always know. Sometimes hope is all we have."

We sit in silence, then I say, "Can I ask you a question?"

"What's on your mind?"

"What made the state church change?"

She looks at me, surprised, then says, "That's complicated."

"I'm fourteen now. I can understand complicated things."

"Well, it didn't happen overnight. It goes back thirty years, to when the Netherlands first gained independence from France. King William made the Reformed church the official state church."

I watch flames flicker in the stove. "That seems like a good thing."

"It does. It did. But the king placed the church under the authority of the state. Always before it was ruled by elders. Their only authority was the word of God and the Reformed confessions. Now the government makes the rules and appoints the leaders."

"Why did the church let that happen?"

"It seemed like a good thing. Our government leaders used tax money to build churches, help the poor, even pay ministers. But with that money came control."

I look at her, surprised. It sounds like something the widow Wolters would say.

"It wasn't obvious, at first," she adds. "But little by little, the officials made changes."

"Like what?"

"They added hymns. We always sang psalms before."

"Are hymns not good?"

"Many are fine. Beautiful even. But others aren't. Salvation is a gift. Some of the hymns make salvation seem like something we can earn. We end up singing what we would never allow our minster to preach."

"What else did they change?"

"Elders used to swear an oath to teach and defend the truths of the Bible as summarized in the Reformed confessions. Now they're free to ignore the confessions or even oppose them."

She dips her fingertip into the milk to test the temperature and invites me to do the same.

"It's ready," she says, and adds a square of rennet. "This comes from the stomach lining of a calf. It makes the milk separate into solid curd and liquid whey."

I stir the mixture with a long wooden paddle. "Start at the bottom," she says, "and work your way up. Nice and slow. In large circles. That's good."

When it's well-mixed, we wrap a large cloth around the top. "To keep out the flies," she says. Together, we move the pot off the stove, but close enough that it stays warm. She smiles. "Now we wait."

I never knew making cheese involved so much waiting.

"This will take some time," she says. "I'm going to make sure Luc is behaving for Mrs. Huizen. Meet me back here in an hour."

Outside the shed, wind breathes in the tall grass, causing it to shimmer in the sunlight. I decide to go for a walk along the canal. Beyond the barley fields, my walk turns into a run. I get as far as the pine grove, which towers over the surrounding fields. Like giants. They bristle with sharp needles like they're guarding a treasure.

What are they hiding? I push through to the center of the grove. No treasure. But it is pretty. Sunlight filters through the branches, landing on a fine lacework of needles.

Here and there, a cone has fallen to the ground. I pick one up and examine it. It's constructed with more precision and skill than the finest jewelry. So I guess there's treasure after all.

Back at home, Mother says it's time to return to the cheese shed. She brings out our family Bible and sets it on one of the shelves. She doesn't explain why.

Together, we remove the cloth from the pot. The curd has formed a thick layer at the top. We each touch it with a finger to test its firmness. It feels like custard.

She takes a long knife down from a hook on the wall. "This is called a harp," she says. She carves through the thick curd from one end of the pot to the other, then hands the harp to me. "Your turn. Just one inch over from mine."

I push the harp through the curd and try to follow the cut she made. While hers is straight and true, mine is crooked and uneven.

"Don't worry how it looks. Just make long, narrow strips."

I carve a dozen lines through the curd. Then she turns the pot, and I cut a series of lines that crisscross the others. This creates a sort of chessboard with dozens of small squares of curd.

She covers the pot again.

"Now we wait." I say it this time, and we both laugh.

She reaches for the Bible. "I've been thinking about what you told me last week. That your friends say our church is all about God and Jesus, but theirs is about being good people and loving their neighbor."

I remember.

"And you said you thought church should be about both."

I nod and wait for her to continue.

"Well," she opens the Bible, "I remembered some verses that talk about that, verses that show how those things are connected. This is Ephesians 2:8–9: 'For by grace are ye saved through faith; and that not of yourselves: it is the gift of God: not of works, lest any man should boast.'"

She turns to me. "Do you see how those verses are all about God? His grace. His gift. And not our works. Not at all."

I nod that I understand.

"That's important," she says. "It gives God all the glory. But then Paul goes on to write in verse 10 that we are God's workmanship, created in Christ Jesus unto good works. That tells us *why* God saves us. So we lay down our lives for others, just as he did for us. That's why your father works so hard to provide for us. That's why you help the widow Wolters. By faith we want to do those things."

She flips to another passage. "This is 2 Timothy 3:15. Paul writes that the holy Scriptures are able to make us wise unto salvation through faith in Christ Jesus."

She lets that sink in, then taps her finger to the place where she read from. "Paul starts with God here too. It's God's word that is able to make us wise unto salvation through faith in Jesus. Only when the apostle has made that clear does he go on to talk about life. And he does go on. In verse 17, he tells us why God saves us, so we are equipped to do good works."

Again, I nod.

"One more." She turns to another passage. "This is Titus 2:14. Paul writes that Jesus gave himself for us, to redeem us from all iniquity and purify unto himself a people, zealous to do good works."

This time, when she pauses, I speak. "It starts with Jesus. He died on the cross to save us from our sins. But he did that so we could love him and also love our neighbor."

"Exactly. We mustn't change that order or think we can have one without the other. We aren't able to do good in our own strength. Not good that pleases God. By nature, our will is bound by sin, dead in sin."

"But Jesus sets us free."

"He does. That's the wonder of it all. He gives us new life. He makes us willing and able to walk in his ways. We still fall into sin. Every day. But by faith, we begin to walk in ways that please him."

The pot has rested long enough. We remove the cloth and pour what used to be milk through a cheese cloth. The whey passes through the cloth, leaving only the curds.

We gather up the corners of the cloth and twist it to squeeze the moisture out of the curds, laying them out on a dry cloth. We use our fingers to break them into smaller bits and mix in some salt.

Finally, we tumble the salted curds into a wooden hoop and place the hoop in a cheese press. As we tighten the press with wooden screws, more moisture dribbles out.

I look at Mother. "Now we wait?"

She smiles. "Now we wait. In fact, that's enough for today. We'll check on it tomorrow."

After she has gone to the house to check on Luc, I go to the barn. I bring Samson an apple and climb up into the loft. I'm fourteen years old now. Old enough to make cheese. Old enough to understand about church things. I'm glad we're going to a church that teaches that Jesus saves us from our sins, *and* that we must love our neighbor.

But I still wish I could invite my friends to church.

Early in the evening, Father and Theo return from the fields. Father asks how the cheese making went, and Mother assures him I'm a good student.

We have ham and potatoes for supper with fresh vegetables from the garden. Delicious.

After supper, Mother excuses herself from the table. When she returns, she's carrying a cake. A birthday cake!

I can't believe it. "How?"

She beams with pleasure at my surprise. "It was Mrs. Huizen's idea. She had some sugar she could spare, so she made it this morning while we were busy in the cheese shed."

It's a cream cake. My favorite. Did I mention that Mrs. Huizen is the nicest person ever?

Mother passes out slices of cake to each of us. "A special treat for a special occasion."

"What's 'cassion?" Luc asks.

"That means not every day," she says. "It's special."

"What's special?"

"Eat," Theo says. "Then you'll understand."

Luc grabs a handful of cake in both fists and mashes them into his mouth. "Yum."

"And now," Mother says, "presents."

I've been trying not to think of presents. We don't have extra money right now.

Still, Father produces a small box, neatly wrapped in simple paper. I pull at the paper, trying not to tear it, but impatient to see what's inside.

New shoes! And not just any shoes. Shiny black church shoes! Like the rich girls wear. I look at Father. "How?"

"We bought them last Christmas, but they were too big for you. You've grown since then."

The shoes fit perfectly! I want to cry. No, I want to dance.

Theo says, "So good."

I turn to him. "Aren't they, though?"

But he's not looking at my shoes. He's biting into a second piece of cake. Rude.

Mother taps him on the arm. "Wasn't there something you wanted to give your sister?"

"Oh, right." He leaves the room and returns with a package. It's oddly shaped and poorly wrapped, but still, another birthday present.

I remove the paper and stare in amazement. It's a woodcarving, with three tree branches carefully interwoven, and on each branch, a starling. He carved it himself, but the whole thing is so complicated and stunning, I can hardly believe it.

"Theo! You're an artist."

"You're welcome."

He even lets me give him a hug.

CHAPTER NINETEEN

Saturday morning, we turn our attention to the coming worship service in Otten. Father announces that he and Theo are going to Mr. Visser's blacksmith shop to sweep the floors and set up chairs.

It sounds like fun. "Can I go?"

Father shakes his head. "No."

"I can sweep."

"Mother needs you here."

Theo hands me a broom. "Since you love it so much."

When the house has been cleaned and cleaned again, Mother turns to her sewing. She puts the finishing touches on my new Sunday dress. "I really wanted to have it ready for your birthday, but there just wasn't time."

I try it on and admire my reflection in the window. "I *love* it. It's so pretty."

She smiles. "Especially on you."

I want to go on wearing it all day, but Mother says no, there's work to be done. I water the flowers while she sweeps the steps. I scrub the floors while she washes the windows. Later, when Luc takes a nap, we both go to the cheese shed and carefully turn each wheel of drying cheese.

When we return to the house, Mother begins to plan Sunday dinner. "We'll have pork and spinach and bread. And last year's potatoes."

I look at her, surprised.

"This is a special occasion," she says. "The church in Wittemeer is very generous, allowing Rev. Hoek to come and help us. And the Meers have shown us beautiful hospitality."

I don't argue. I look forward to a proper dinner. "Did you talk to Johannah's mother about coming to church tomorrow? And Nellie's?"

"Yes."

"And?"

"They said they'd consider it."

"Do you think they'll come?"

She looks doubtful. Then her face brightens. "You've made a nice friend in Wittemeer. Annika, right?"

"Yes."

"Good friends are important. You know..." She pauses. "I've lost friends too."

I don't like the way she says "too." As if we've both lost friends. I haven't lost any friends. I just have to work harder to keep them.

But after a moment, her words strike even deeper. Mother has lost friends. And she feels the hurt. I didn't even know she could feel that way. She never shows it.

Sunday morning, everyone wakes early. Mother sets out breakfast. Father paces back and forth, drinking his coffee. Even Theo is up, though his hair is still a mess.

I stand where the sunlight shines through the window, letting it fall on my new dress.

Father sets down his cup. "Where are my good shoes?"

Mother doesn't answer. If it was me or Theo, she'd suggest we look where we left them.

Theo shovels two large pieces of gingerbread into his mouth and makes a face at Luc. "Look. I'm a squirrel."

Luc laughs like it's the funniest thing ever. He looks at me. "Do a rabbit!"

I wrinkle my nose and twitch imaginary whiskers.

He laughs hysterically. "Do a mouse!"

He'll go on like this all day if no one stops him. I say, "We don't have time this morning."

"There's no hurry," Mother says. "Church doesn't begin until ten o'clock."

I frown. "Why so late?"

"Rev. Hoek has to travel all the way from Wittemeer."

When Mother and Father leave the room, Theo says, "That's not the only reason. Uncle Ed thinks there might be trouble with people from the state church."

"What's trouble?" Luc asks.

Theo pokes him in the belly. "*You're* trouble."

A chill runs through me. "What kind of trouble?"

"You *know* there's going to be trouble."

"Well, how do we avoid it?"

"I don't know. Leave the Netherlands."

I roll my eyes. "You're always looking for excuses to go to America."

"Maybe. But that *is* why we're meeting late. So that the state church will already be meeting by the time we get to town."

"What about after church?"

He shrugs. "Hopefully they go home."

"What if they don't?"

"Trouble." He gets up and leaves the room.

Luc looks at me. "What's trouble?"

"Nothing," I say quickly. "Theo's just teasing." I wish it was true.

By the time we set out for Otten, the sun is well overhead. We walk in silence, arriving in town just as the state church is beginning their service. The streets are empty.

132

A pang of guilt hits me as we pass the Brugplatz. Cobie is there, probably watching from the window. But what can I do? My friends will be at church. Annika is coming all the way from Wittemeer. I have to be there to welcome them. I can't do everything.

At the blacksmith's shop, I hurry inside.

Annika jumps up when she sees me, and we hug in the aisle. She says, "You have a new dress. It's so pretty."

I hold out my foot so she can see my shoes as well. We both laugh and hug again.

She says, "I have to tell you something after church."

"Tell me now."

She shakes her head. "After church."

Betsie leaves her seat along the far wall and joins us. "Tess, I love your dress."

"Thank you."

"It's nicer than anything Eva has."

It isn't true, but she's nice to say it.

"Come, sit by me."

I shake my head. "You sit by me. Close to the door so we don't miss our friends when they arrive."

After a quick chat with Uncle Ed, she returns. "I may sit with you," she lowers her voice to mimic Uncle Ed's, "*if we behave.*"

Annika gets permission to sit with us as well.

I keep both eyes on the door. "Who do you think will come first?"

Betsie shrugs.

The door opens and I jump to my feet. False alarm. Mr. and Mrs. van Til amble inside. They're an older couple who live across the street from the blacksmith's shop.

I ask Betsie, "Do you think Julia will come, even if her parents don't approve?"

"No."

"She might."

"Would you go to the state church against your parents' wishes?"

"I guess not."

The door opens again. I lean forward.

Mrs. de Voort enters the room. She's a widow who lives with her daughter's family out beyond the canal. She's alone.

A few more people arrive, but they're mostly old.

I turn to Betsie. "Do people even know we're meeting here? Do they know we're starting at ten o'clock?" The room feels empty. Annika's family. Uncle Ed. The Kosters. And a few other families, but none of my friends.

At ten o'clock, Rev. Hoek makes his way to a makeshift wooden pulpit. He opens with prayer, and we sing an opening psalm. He reads from Hebrews 11, where Abraham leaves his home and travels to a land that God would give him as an inheritance.

To be honest, I don't hear much of the sermon. I'm still thinking about my friends. No Julia. No Susannah. And where are Johannah and Nellie?

Finally, Rev. Hoek says, "Amen," and we sing a closing psalm. It isn't even one of my favorites.

I turn to Betsie. "I don't understand. No one came."

Betsie looks unconcerned. "They never said they'd come."

I hate the way she says it. Like she knew all along. "You didn't even *want* them to come."

"I did. I..." Tears show in her eyes.

I don't care. I'm in no mood to apologize. My friends have abandoned me. I burst out into the street. The sun is bright, and my eyes take a moment to adjust.

Annika follows me out. "Don't be sad."

"No one came."

"This is just what happened in Wittemeer the first week. But look how many people come now."

"But how do you know—" I stop short.

On the far side of the street, a group of people is gathered. Members of the state church, and they don't look happy.

Theo elbows me. "Trouble."

Father, Mother, and Luc emerge into the sunshine, but stop when they notice the people across the street.

Mr. Jonkeer steps forward. "What's the meaning of this gathering?" He turns to Rev. Hoek. "Who are you?"

"I'm Rev. Hoek." He extends his hand. "Pastor in the new Reformed church in Wittemeer."

Mr. Jonkeer ignores his hand. "What are you doing in Otten?"

"Feeding the flock."

"You're not welcome here. Go back to Wittemeer."

"That's what I intend." He motions to the rest of us. "Return home. We don't want trouble."

I don't see any of my friends among the people gathered across the street. That's a relief. But Julia's younger brothers are there, standing next to her father.

The oldest, Louis, steps into the street and shouts, "Dogs!"

I'd like to strangle him. But Father and Mother ignore him and turn toward home. So do the others.

"That's right," Louis shouts. "Go home, scolds!"

I turn to follow my parents, but after just a few steps, something strikes me hard in the back of my head. I spin around.

"Ha!" Louis points and laughs. His hands are filthy.

I put a hand to the back of my head. It comes away wet and slimy. Manure! It clings to my bonnet. It's running down my hair, staining my new dress.

Mr. Jonkeer puts a hand on Louis' shoulder. "That's enough of that." But there's laughter in his eyes.

Louis ignores him. He stoops down to pick up more manure.

Before he can throw it, a clod of manure strikes him in the face. He yelps and falls over backward, crying and clawing at his eyes.

Mr. Jonkeer's fine gray suit is splattered with manure as well. He swells with rage. "Why you little..."

I turn to see who threw it. Kohl. From Wittemeer. What's he doing in Otten?

Theo grins at Kohl and mimics Mr. Jonkeer's voice. *"That's enough of that."*

Kohl's eyes meet mine. Then he looks away.

I remember what I must look like—manure clinging to my hair and dress. I turn and run. I kick off my new Sunday shoes and run barefoot. I flee across the bridge and don't stop until I get home. Then, down the path beyond the barn, I fling myself into the canal.

Dousing myself, I shake my head furiously. Manure darkens the water, washing downstream in the current.

Item by item, I remove my outer clothing. Someone might see me, but really, what's more shameful than manure in your hair and all down your dress?

In the bushes, a starling begins to sing. I don't want to hear it. Sundays are nothing like heaven. They're hard and cruel and wicked.

I sink to my knees, letting the water wash over me. Maybe Theo is right. Maybe the only way to avoid trouble is to cross the nearest ocean. If I had enough money, I would get on a ship this very afternoon. No, not on Sunday. But first thing Monday. No, I'd have to say goodbye to Cobie first. But Tuesday. I would leave forever on Tuesday.

CHAPTER TWENTY

The water in the canal is cold, even in August. I soon find myself shivering. I gather up my clothes and go inside the house.

When Mother returns from church, she finds me in bed, buried under my blankets. She sets out a fresh change of clothes.

I tell her, "I'm never leaving this room."

She coaxes my head out from under the covers and runs a brush through my hair. "Annika will be here soon."

"It's so embarrassing."

"Friends don't mind a little embarrassment."

Voices come from the other room. Mother says, "That'll be the Meers. Shall I send Annika in?"

I glance around my room. What a mess. Mother took my wet clothes away, but yesterday's clothes are still slung across the back of my bed.

Mother returns to the kitchen, and a few moments later Annika knocks on my door. She opens it a crack. "Tess? I brought your shoes."

"Thank you. Come in."

She sets them down by the door. "Betsie found them. She asked me to bring them to you. Are you alright?"

"I'm fine. Just ashamed."

"It's that boy who should be ashamed. If it makes you feel any better, he was crying like a baby when I left."

I shouldn't admit it, but it does make me feel better. I ask her, "How did Kohl get to Otten?"

"I don't know."

I change into the clothes Mother brought me. "All my friends will hear about this. They might even laugh."

She gives me a quick hug. "I don't believe that. Not friends."

"I really hoped some of them would come to church this morning."

"I know you did."

"Especially Julia."

"I hoped to meet her."

"I should have known better. Her father is an elder in the state church. He says their church is more loving than ours. Do you think that's true?"

"Well, they weren't very loving today, were they?"

"No. But I'm not feeling very loving either."

"Love is more than just a feeling. It means giving of yourself to help other people, even when that means sacrifice."

It's true, I know. But who can I help? I'm barely fourteen. Cobie, but that's complicated. I know what she needs, but how can I help with that?

Mother knocks on my door. "Girls? Dinner is ready."

Annika clasps my hands. "My mother brought pudding."

"Is that what you wanted to tell me at church?"

"No. That's different. I'll tell you after dinner."

In the dining room, the others are already seated at the table. Rev. Hoek is there. And the Meers. Annika's little brothers are trying to get Luc to say "yum."

We open with prayer, and everyone begins to eat. Everyone but me. I'm not hungry.

Father passes Rev. Hoek a basket of bread. "I'm sorry you had to deal with Mr. Jonkeer. We hoped to avoid trouble by starting later."

"It's alright," he replies. "I just feel bad for Tess."

I stare at my plate, hoping someone changes the subject.

Rev. Hoek refills his water. "I'd like to come and lead another service for you. But perhaps you should find another meeting place first."

Father nods. "I'm sure we can do that."

I hold my breath. Please, not in a barn.

Mother says, "We hoped more of our neighbors would join us. A few came, but there are so many who didn't."

"We also started small," Mrs. Meers says. "But each week we continue to grow."

They talk about church things all through dinner. Then Mother sets out the Meers' pudding, and everyone enjoys dessert. I barely touched my dinner, but I can't resist the pudding. It's delicious.

After dinner, Mr. Meers asks Father, "Are you familiar with Rev. van Raalte?"

"Yes. He's the minister over in Arnhem."

"He wrote this." He hands Father a pamphlet. "Have you seen it?"

Father glances at it and frowns. "I've seen it."

"He gives fifty pages of well-reasoned arguments for going to America. Is it something you've considered?"

"No."

"Why not?"

"I'm a poor farmer. I don't suppose I'll be going anywhere."

"Lots of poor farmers are going."

Father shakes his head. "If the day ever comes that I go to America, it will be for freedom of worship, not financial gain."

Theo's been listening, but now he joins in. "Maybe people who are able to work their own land and build a future are better able to protect their freedoms."

I hate to admit it, but I see his point. Sometimes spiritual things and earthly things get all tangled together.

But Father isn't moved. "God made me a Hollander, and a Hollander I shall remain."

Mr. Meers smiles. "Let's test that logic. If someone offered you a job with better wages, would you take it?"

"I'm not sure I understand."

"Would you reject it on principle?"

"On what principle?"

"On the principle that God made you a poor farmer, and a poor farmer you will remain."

"I see," Father huffs. "You make a point."

"And when you met your wife, did you say 'God made me single, and single I will remain'?"

"Alright, you win. Nonetheless, I will remain where God planted me."

"Fair enough." Mr. Meers glances at his wife. "I don't know that this is the time for such an announcement, but...I've decided to join Rev. van Raalte."

I stare at him. "You're going to Arnhem?"

Mother gives me a look. The one that says, "Don't interrupt adult conversation." I usually mind Mother's looks, but this is important.

"Not Arnhem," Mr. Meers says. "America."

"For how long?"

"To stay."

I stare at him. "Who will take care of your family?"

He chuckles. "I'm bringing them with me. We're *all* going to America."

I turn to Annika.

Her eyes are filled with pain. "That's what I was going to tell you."

I feel like I've been kicked in the stomach. My old friends have abandoned me. Now Annika is forsaking me too?

I want to leave the table. I want to run away. But conversation continues all around me.

"What about your business?" Father asks.

"I have an apprentice, a capable young man. His father has agreed to take it over."

140

"You haven't spoken of this before."

"I hoped to stay, but the authorities in Wittemeer have made it clear they'll continue to make life difficult. I hope your city leaders are more supportive than ours."

Theo chokes on his milk, nearly snorting it out of his nose. Disgusting, but understandable. No one expects Mr. Everhart to be especially supportive.

Father turns to Rev. Hoek. "You approve of this? Leaving our homeland?"

Rev. Hoek sighs. "My father served as a deacon in one of the first groups to leave the state church. Ten years ago, when I was about Theo's age, armed soldiers broke up our meeting. Authorities fined my father a hundred guilders. For being a deacon. For helping the poor! When he couldn't pay, they sold our things, auctioned them off on a Sunday so none of our friends could buy them back for us. When that wasn't enough, they put him in prison. We were so ashamed. My mother cried herself to sleep for a month."

"I'm sorry," Father says. "That's terrible."

"Later, government officials forced us to house a dozen soldiers in our home. In our tiny little home! We had to give them our beds and sleep on the floor. We had to feed them and wash their clothes and listen to their filthy talk, their crude remarks about my sisters."

Mother covers her mouth with her hand. "How horrible."

"And cruel," Rev. Hoek adds. "They told us the soldiers were necessary to protect us from the mob. But really, they were just another way to make our lives miserable."

Father frowns. "But surely things have gotten better since then. No one is being thrown into prison today."

"True," Rev. Hoek says, "but we have no more legal right to meet than our parents did then. We have freedom only at the whim of the king. If he changes his mind, or if the next king feels differently..."

Father opens his mouth to respond, then closes it again.

I wonder what Mother is thinking. Does she want to stay in the Netherlands or go to America? She's never said. All she says now is, "Perhaps we should close so the children can get away from the table."

When Annika and I are outside, she says, "I'm sorry. I wanted to tell you."

"You can't leave. You're my friend."

Tears show in her eyes, and that brings them to mine. I tell her, "My old friends hardly talk to me now. You're my *only* friend. You and Betsie. We'll never see each other again!"

"I know. Unless—"

"Of course!" I interrupt her. "We have to convince your parents to stay."

She shakes her head. "We should convince *your* parents to come with us."

Maybe she's right, but it doesn't matter. Father will never leave the Netherlands. I guess it will be just Betsie and me from now on. It's a good thing God made cousins. With Betsie, I can survive anything.

CHAPTER TWENTY-ONE

L ater that afternoon, Father hitches Samson to our wagon, and we travel to Wittemeer for the evening service.

Once again, the street outside the church building is bustling with wagons and carriages. But this time, there's a feeling of chaos and disorder. As we get closer, I see why. Officers in uniforms block the doorway.

I spot Uncle Ed across the way. He's out of his wagon, and arguing with one of the officers.

Mr. Meers approaches our wagon. "They're shutting down our worship service. They say our building is too small for all the people who come now."

Father looks concerned. "What will you do?"

"One of our members has volunteered the use of his property."

An officer overhears him and interrupts. "If you attempt to gather somewhere else, we'll shut that down as well. There must be an inspection for size and ventilation."

Mr. Meers laughs. "It's the Waals' north property—ten acres of rolling meadow. Feel free to inspect it, but I assure you it's well ventilated."

The officer's face reddens, and he stalks off.

"Where is this property?" Father asks. "Can I give you a ride?"

"Yes. Thank you."

"What about your family?"

"They've already gone ahead."

Mother slides over to make room for Mr. Meers, and we join a parade of buggies and wagons rolling into the countryside north of Wittemeer.

Father turns to Mr. Meers. "Your officials gave you no warning of this?"

He shakes his head. "From the beginning they've threatened to shut us down but gave no warning it would happen today."

"And they still haven't given you permission to find a larger space?"

"No. First, we were too few. Now, we're too many."

North of Wittemeer, Mr. Meers motions to a grassy meadow. "Here."

Father draws Samson up at the side of the road.

Mr. Meers steps down. "We'll set up a pulpit here in the draw. You can find a seat anywhere on that hillside."

Father and Theo offer to stay behind and help others who are still arriving. Mother helps Luc down from the wagon, and I gather up some quilts for us to sit on.

The meadow rises gently to our left. Thankfully, there are no cows. Just crickets, which leap from the tall grass as we pass.

Halfway up the hill, Mother stops to say hello to the Kosters and the Vissers. I continue on and find myself face to face with Kohl. I've been hoping to run into him, but I'm caught off guard. All I manage to say is, "Hello."

"Hello," he says. "I hope you don't mind meeting outside."

"Not at all." I hesitate, then add, "I wanted to thank you for standing up to Louis this morning."

His face reddens. "I probably shouldn't have done that...but he shouldn't have done that either."

"Well, thank you. How did you get to Otten, anyway?"

"I...well, I better go help direct traffic." He turns and walks away.

Nearby, I find Annika and Betsie waiting for me. Annika smiles slyly. "I saw you talking to Kohl."

Now *my* face turns red. "I just wanted to thank him for this morning. And ask how he got to Otten and back."

"Did he give you an answer?"

"No."

She smiles. "He's not very generous with his life story."

Theo joins us, stretching out in the grass. He snaps off a long stem and pops one end in his mouth. "This is how church should be."

Annika smiles sweetly.

Once again, I have to be the practical one. "What about winter?"

"Enough about winter," he scoffs. "Why are you always worrying about winter? It's August."

The sun casts a warm light over the slope. A deer steps into the meadow, eyes the strange assortment of visitors, and slips back into the trees.

Down below, the elders are ready to begin. Rev. Hoek steps behind a makeshift pulpit, basically a wooden crate placed on a bale of hay. He opens with prayer and begins the worship service just as if we're all seated in a proper church.

He preaches from John 15:12-13, "This is my commandment, That ye love one another, as I have loved you. Greater love hath no man than this, that a man lay down his life for his friends." Jesus laid down his life for his friends. We're called to show that same kind of love. He asks how we can make sacrifices for the good of our friends.

I wish I had a good answer, but I'm only fourteen.

Rev. Hoek reads from Luke 10, where Jesus tells the story of the good Samaritan. He asks how we can be the kind of neighbor God wants us to be.

I've always liked that story, but again, I'm only fourteen. What can I do?

He reads from James 1, which says that visiting the fatherless and widows in their troubles is pure religion and undefiled before God.

I do know a widow.

And a fatherless person.

But I already visit them. What else can I do?

When Rev. Hoek says, "Amen," we all stand to sing the final psalm. It's beautiful, all of us standing together, surrounded by meadow, and the sun sinking low.

Afterward I see Mari, *that* Mari, standing on the ridge above, silhouetted against a soft sky. Theo sees her too. He brushes himself off and says, "I should...help people find their way back to their wagons."

Annika watches him go. "He's so nice."

I give her a look. "Too bad you'll be off in America, and he'll be here with Betsie and me."

Betsie clears her throat. "Um..."

"Um, what?"

She raises her eyes, and I see she's been crying. "I might have to go to America too."

I stare at her.

"Just on the way here, Father told me he thinks we should go." She glances at Annika. "I think Mr. Meers convinced him."

"You can't. I need you!"

"I know. You're my best friend." She blinks back tears. "I begged."

A chill runs through me. "What's wrong with everyone? Why is everyone in such a hurry to leave?"

"I want to stay," she says. "I told him I want to stay here with you."

"Why does *he* want to go?"

"He says we have to think about the future. He doesn't think Mr. Everhart will ever allow us to start a Christian school."

Tears burn the corners of my eyes as she reaches to hug me. Why is this happening? Why would God take away my best friend?

Annika stands silently by, the color drained from her face. I reach a hand and draw her into our embrace. We stand that way, three girls, arm in arm, tears streaming down our faces. Not pretty tears either. Awful, shoulder-wrenching, nose-running tears.

Finally, Betsie speaks. "What if you can go too? Maybe my father can convince yours."

I close my eyes and squeeze my friends tighter. Maybe. If anyone can change Father's mind, it's Uncle Ed. But I don't think it will happen.

Back at the wagon, Theo takes one look at me and says, "You've been crying."

"So?"

"I guess you heard." His face is so calm. *He* wants to go to America more than anyone, but he puts up with Father's hesitance with no anger, no bitterness, no tears. How does he do it?

When Father and Mother and Luc return to the wagon, we all climb in and turn toward home.

As soon as we're out of Wittemeer, I climb up between Father and Mother. "Can we talk?"

"Of course," Father says.

"Uncle Ed told Betsie he wants to go to America."

"He told me the same thing."

"And that doesn't bother you?"

"He has to decide what's best for them."

My tears start again. "Betsie's my best friend."

Mother takes my hand in hers. "We know, dear."

"Maybe we should go with them." Before Father can give reasons for staying, I add, "Maybe we're just being stubborn."

Normally that would draw a rebuke from Mother. It probably should. But she only squeezes my hand.

Father presses his lips together but doesn't respond.

Theo speaks up from the back. "Maybe we should put it up to a vote."

No one takes that seriously. But it makes me wonder how the vote would turn out. Theo wants to go. Father wants to stay. Mother doesn't say what she thinks. At least not to me. Up until today, I wanted to stay. But not without Betsie.

That leaves Luc, who doesn't even understand. But maybe Luc is the key. With all his questions, what kind of answers will he learn in school if we stay here in Otten?

I turn to Father, trying to make my voice sound less angry than I feel. "Do you think about the future?"

He clears his throat. "I do. I try to. Next Sunday, Rev. Hoek is coming to Otten again to lead another worship service, so that's good."

That's not what I meant by the future. And I'm not even sure it's good. This morning certainly didn't end well.

"The evening service this time," he says. "Hopefully, more people will come."

"At the blacksmith shop?"

"No."

A shiver runs down my back. "In the barn?"

He shakes his head. "No cows. The Kosters have offered the use of their dry goods store. But don't tell anyone. We don't want any more trouble."

That's one thing we can agree on. We don't want any more trouble.

CHAPTER TWENTY-TWO

Tuesday morning, I make my way to town. At the Brugplatz, the widow Wolters ushers me inside. "You're early."

"Sorry. I didn't want to be late."

"Very well."

I exchange hellos with Cobie and turn my attention to the mantel in the other room. The widow follows me. "I heard there was an incident at your church service."

"I'd rather not talk about it."

"Come, now." Her eyes glitter with curiosity. She has no intention of dropping the matter. "I heard little Louis Jonkeer was involved."

The mention of his name makes my breath catch. "It was nothing. Just a boy being foolish."

She frowns. "Don't make excuses for him. He's a rat."

I look up. I'm surprised she even knows him. "He *is* a rat. But his father would have done the same thing if he thought he could get away with it."

She smiles grimly. "Aren't we just the pride of Otten."

I go back to cleaning and refuse to answer any more questions about the incident.

She takes down her cane. "I have an appointment with my lawyers today."

"Alright."

"I'll be gone a couple of hours."

"Alright."

When she's gone and the mantel is clean, Cobie asks, "What was that about your church service?"

"Nothing." Cobie's never been to church, and I've only told her good things about it. I don't want her to know church members can treat each other so badly. It seems shameful.

She makes her way to the window. Her foot seems better. She still limps but doesn't need any help. She eases into a chair. "What I really want, more than anything, is to go outside."

"I know."

"But I really, really, really want to. We could go right now. I wouldn't tell." Her dark eyes glitter with mischief.

"Sorry. I made a bargain with your aunt. She won't allow it."

"Except on Sundays," she says.

"But I go to church on Sundays."

"You could take me with you."

"You know she won't allow that."

We sit in silence for several minutes. I remember Rev. Hoek's sermon in the rolling meadow north of Wittemeer. Visiting the fatherless is "pure religion and undefiled." But Cobie needs so much more than a visit. She needs to get outside, to feel the sun on her face, to hear the birds sing.

She's as close to the man in Jesus' story as anyone I'm likely to meet. Am I the priest who crosses over to the other side of the road? The Levite who does the same? Or the good Samaritan who binds up her wounds?

But what can I do? I'd have to stay home from church on a Sunday morning. I almost tell her I'll do it but stop just in time. It's impossible. My parents will never allow it.

"Which one is the church?" Cobie asks. "Can we see it from here?"

"There." I point to where the bell tower rises against the sky.

"Oh." She admires it. "It's taller than the other buildings."

I tell her about the stone steps and the big oak doors. "And inside, it has lots of benches for people to sit on, and tall windows to let in the light."

"I wish I could go with you."

"Me too." I don't explain that I no longer go to that church, that I travel all the way to Wittemeer and worship in a church that isn't even a church. Or in a farmer's field.

She looks at me with her beautiful, dark eyes. "What do you do at church?"

"We sing. And see our friends. And the minister teaches us things from the Bible."

"What kind of things?"

"Things. Stories."

"I like stories. Tell me a church story."

"Alright." I tell her one of my favorites. "A long time ago, there was a drought in the land. That means there wasn't any rain for a long time. During that time, God sent a prophet named Elijah to the city of Zarephath. When he came to the gate, he saw a widow gathering sticks."

"Aunt Ruth is a widow."

"Right. But this widow was poor. The prophet asked her to bring him a little water, so he could drink. And a piece of bread. She told him she had no bread—only a handful of flour and a little oil. She was gathering sticks to start a fire. She would make the last of her flour into a meal for herself and her son. Then they would have nothing more to eat and would probably die."

Cobie looks at me. "I don't like sad stories."

"This one gets better," I assure her. "Elijah told the widow not to be afraid—to make a small loaf of bread for him and then make something for herself and her son. God would make it so her jar of flour

151

would not be used up and her jug of oil would not run dry until he sent rain again."

I pause, but Cobie says, "Go on."

"The widow did what Elijah told her and found that every day there was food for herself and her son, just as Elijah had said. God made it so that her flour was never used up and her oil never ran dry."

"That's a good story. Tell me another."

"I should have brought my Bible storybook. A friend gave it to me for my birthday."

"You had a birthday?"

"On Friday."

"I wish I'd known. I'd have made you something."

"You don't have to make me anything."

"I want to. You're my friend."

I'm glad she thinks of me as her friend. I want to be her friend. Not because I made a bargain with the widow. Not because she pays me. Because Cobie *needs* a friend, and I'm the only one who can help her. And I'm happy to do it.

"Maybe I can bring the storybook with me on Thursday."

She claps her hands. "But tell me another story now. From memory."

I tell her about Moses and Pharaoh, about Rahab and the walls of Jericho, about Daniel and the lions' den.

After each story, she sighs with satisfaction. Sometimes she asks a question. Sometimes she asks lots of questions. But in the end, she says, "I like these stories."

"They're not *just* stories," I say. "They really happened. They teach us about God and how much he loves us."

She nods that she understands.

When the widow returns, she asks, "What have you two been talking about?"

"We..." I hesitate.

Cobie says, "We were talking about lions. But they didn't eat anyone."

The widow raises an eyebrow but says nothing.

Later, she sends Cobie off to do her lessons, and I get up to clean the other mantel.

"Stay." She waves me back.

I hesitate, then sit down. My friends will be gathering at the well soon. If I'm late, I might miss them. But it seems the widow wants to talk. Visiting widows is pure religion and undefiled. I can stay a few minutes.

She says, "Sometimes I get tired of this town. When I was married, we'd often go abroad. London. Rome. Cairo, even."

"How long has your husband been gone?" Too late, I realize that might be a rude question. Sometimes I blurt things out without thinking them through. It's one of my worst faults.

But she doesn't get angry. "Twelve years. We were very happy together. Not all married people are, you know. I helped him with his business. He introduced me to interesting people. We had friends in Amsterdam and the Hague. We went to wonderful parties." She practically glows as she recalls the good times.

After a long pause, she says, "When he died, my family thought it best to let my brother take over my finances. He promised to take care of me, of course, but as soon as the paperwork was signed, he hid me away in the shoddiest apartment he could find."

"One of your own."

"Well...yes."

"And Cobie?"

"Ah, Cobie. She came a couple of years later. After his...well, you should know my brother is not a moral man. I agreed to take her in if he agreed to give me back control of my finances. Our little business arrangement."

"Is that when you left the church?"

"They knew he was no good. They must have. And yet they made him an elder. I couldn't stay."

I can see she's upset with him, but what about her own actions? She keeps Cobie hidden away and won't let her go outside. Just so she can control her own finances.

The clock strikes twelve, and I can't wait any longer. I excuse myself and clean the mantel in the other room, then hurry to the door.

I'm late getting to the well, but my friends are still there. Well, two of them—Julia and Eva.

Julia gives me a hug. "The others wanted to come, but Nellie's sick, and...well, you know how busy summertime can be."

I nod as if I understand.

Eva doesn't bother to hug me. She says, "I can't stay, but I did want to hear about the trouble over at your church."

Julia grasps my hand. "We heard what happened. How horrid."

I'm too ashamed to say anything.

Julia apologizes for Louis. "He didn't mean anything. He's just little. My father was very disappointed in him."

I know better. I saw laughter on Mr. Jonkeer's face. And approval too. But Julia doesn't need to know that.

"My father says he could have had your minister arrested," Eva says. "But he chose not to because your church is too small and insignificant to bother about."

Thankfully, Julia changes the subject. "Old Mr. Steyn fell asleep at our church. He snored so loud his wife had to poke him. Then he jumped and shouted something about French soldiers massing at the border."

Eva laughs. "I don't know why he even comes to church. Last week, he nearly fell just getting out of his carriage."

They tell me all the news from town, but our conversation feels awkward and forced.

Finally, Eva says, "My mother baked a peach cobbler this morning, if you want to come over."

She knows Julia loves peach cobbler. And she knows I won't go.

"I'm not hungry," Julia says. "Let's go to the schoolhouse and play shuffleboard."

Eva scrunches her face. "I hurt my wrist. And I can't stay anyway. We're getting rid of some things today. Baby things too. Maybe you can find something for little Marianne."

Julia's eyes light up, but she says, "Maybe later. I want to talk to Tess first."

"Don't be *too* long, or the best things will be gone." Eva skips away.

Julia turns back to me. "Is your church going to meet again on Sunday?"

"Yes."

"Isn't that dangerous?" She lowers her voice. "Eva said her father won't have anyone arrested, but that's not what I heard. Couldn't you meet somewhere else? Someplace secret?"

Concern shows in her eyes. I love her for that. I tell her, "We won't meet at the blacksmith's shop again."

"Oh, good." Then she says, "It's kind of exciting, isn't it?"

"No." I shake my head. "It's horrid."

CHAPTER TWENTY-THREE

Thursday morning, I prepare to go to town. I promised Cobie I'd bring my Bible storybook, but now I have second thoughts. If Mother sees me with it, she'll ask questions. Why bring a children's storybook to a widow's house? And one who doesn't even go to church?

But Cobie is looking forward to it, so I take a chance and sneak it out of the house.

At the Brugplatz, the widow spots it immediately. "What's this?"

"A storybook."

She takes it from me. "A *Bible* storybook." She thumbs through it, then looks up. "A gift for us?"

That catches me by surprise. She doesn't even seem angry. I didn't intend to give the book to Cobie, but I feel foolish admitting that now. Annika gave it to me because we're friends. And Cobie is my friend too. Shouldn't I be willing to give it to her? And the widow seems so pleased. I hear myself say yes.

She flips through more pages. "It's really ours? We don't have to return it when we're done?"

I nod.

"How thoughtful." She walks over to the dustbin and tosses the book into it. "We're done."

Her eyes flash with satisfaction. She folds her arms and waits for me to explode.

I want to explode, believe me. But I have no intention of giving her what she wants. I choke back my anger, brush past her, and start to clean her mantel. I'm tempted to break her Delft plate over my knee. No, over her head.

She watches me work. "You needn't be offended. It isn't God I disapprove of. Just the church."

When I don't respond, she says, "If you knew my brother, you'd understand."

Still, I ignore her.

When she realizes I'm not going to argue with her, she changes the subject. "I have some errands to run this morning. I'll be back after eleven o'clock."

I finish cleaning the mantel and wait until she leaves, then sit down, exhausted.

Cobie joins me. "She's not always like that. Don't be angry."

"I'm not angry."

"Your hands are."

I look down at my hands, which are clenched into fists. Alright, I *am* angry. But I have a right to be. I'd actually begun to like the widow. I even thought we were becoming friends.

Cobie pulls my book out of the bin and hands it to me. "Read."

We sit down by the window, and I flip through the pages. She stops me at an engraving of soldiers. "This one."

I start at the top of the page. "A long time ago, the army of Ben-Hadad, king of Syria, laid siege to the city of Samaria. The walls of the city kept the soldiers out, but the army camped outside the gates and kept people from going in or out. Farmers couldn't get to their fields. Storekeepers couldn't get supplies. Soon food ran low. Rich people offered lots of money for the scraps that remained. Then even the scraps were gone. People were starving."

"Is this a sad story?"

"It gets better. I promise. Elisha, a prophet from God, told Samaria to trust God. He told them that the very next day, they'd be able to buy flour for only a nickel and barley for a penny.

"An officer of the king refused to believe Elisha. He mocked the prophet, saying that was impossible. Elisha told the officer that he would see the food with his own eyes, but he wouldn't get to eat any of it."

I pause and look at Cobie.

Her eyes are wide, but she says, "Keep reading."

"That night, God caused the Syrian soldiers to hear the sound of chariots and horses and a great army. Afraid that another army was marching to protect the city, they ran for their lives. They fled in such a hurry that they left their tents and all their supplies behind."

"The next morning, the people of Samaria discovered that the soldiers had fled. They went into the soldiers' tents and found all the food they could eat. There was so much food that flour sold for a nickel and barley for a penny. Just as Elisha had told them."

Cobie claps her hands.

"Wait. There's more." I read the last paragraph. "As the people rushed to get the food, they accidentally trampled to death an officer of the king who was guarding the gate. It was the same officer who had mocked Elisha the day before. He saw the food with his own eyes but didn't get to eat any of it."

Cobie looks at me. "That's in the Bible?"

"It is."

"Was there really another army?"

"No. God just made them hear those sounds."

"I thought so. Tell me another."

Flipping through the book, I find another favorite. We read the story of Joseph being sold into slavery by his brothers.

"One more," Cobie says.

We read about Joseph and Potiphar's wife.

"One more."

We read about Pharaoh's dreams, Joseph's interpretation, and how Pharaoh made Joseph ruler in Egypt.

"One more."

We read how famine came to the land of Canaan, how Jacob sent Joseph's brothers to Egypt to buy grain, how Joseph recognized them.

Just after Joseph revealed himself to his brothers, Cobie puts her hand on my arm. The widow has reappeared in the lane, making her way back home.

Cobie says, "Put the storybook back in the bin. I'll get it out later, when she forgets about it. I promise."

The widow enters the room and immediately checks the bin. Satisfied, she turns to us and finds us chatting quietly.

It's almost noon, so I excuse myself to clean the mantel in the other room. When I return, she hands me a ten-guilder note and says, "We'll see you next week."

I turn to the door, but I can't leave without saying something. "What you did was horrid."

"Was it?" She shrugs. "I can be horrid sometimes. Ask anyone."

"I was trying to do something nice for Cobie."

"You know better than to bring that book here. That was never part of the bargain."

Bargain! I'm so sick of that word. She uses it like a weapon. Well, I can do that too. I gather my courage. "I'll be back on Sunday morning."

She narrows her eyes. "For what purpose?"

"To take Cobie outside."

Cobie sits up, her eyes bright.

The widow shakes her head. "I can't allow that."

"You made a bargain."

"It's impossible. Besides, you'll be in church."

"I'll skip church."

"Your parents won't allow it."

It's true, I know. But one look at Cobie and I know I have to find a way. It's what the good Samaritan would do. It's what a friend would do. "I'll be here at half past nine."

I turn and leave before the widow can object.

At home, I climb into the loft and retrieve my savings from the gap in the rafters. I add the ten guilders the widow gave me today. Then I sit down to think. How can I convince Father and Mother to let me stay home from church? If I pretend to be sick, Mother will insist on staying home with me. Still, there has to be a way. Cobie needs help. And no one else can do it. I'm her only friend. No one else even knows she exists.

I lay out my savings, just to look at them. Eighty guilders. Already a fortune. By Christmas, I'll have more than two hundred. I could use some of that to buy presents. For Mother, a pair of fancy bracelets like Mrs. Borgman wears. For Theo, a new knife for whittling.

And something for Luc. But what?

What he really needs is the chance to go to a good Christian school. And Theo doesn't really need a new knife. He needs a chance to work his own land and not spend his whole life working for the likes of Mr. Borgman. But money can't buy those things. At least, not in the Netherlands.

Suddenly, Theo calls from the foot of the ladder. "Tess? What are you doing up there?"

I scramble to gather up the money at my feet. "Nothing."

The ladder creaks as he climbs its rungs. "What do you mean, nothing?"

"Nothing!" I stuff the money into the burlap sack and jam it into the gap in the rafters.

His head appears at the top of the ladder as the sack tumbles back out of its secret hiding place. It hits the floor, and a flurry of banknotes flutter out.

He gapes at the money. "What's this?"

"Let me explain."

"You robbed the bank?"

"If I tell you, you have to promise not to tell anyone."

"Where'd you get all this money?"

It's too late for secrets. I tell Theo about the widow, how her tiny apartment isn't so tiny. How the noises we heard that day were no cat. I even tell him about Cobie. To be honest, I'm relieved. I've kept it to myself too long.

He looks at me in disbelief. "No one else knows?"

"Doctor Brink knows."

"And he keeps it secret too?"

"There might be others. She knows how to keep people quiet."

"And she won't let this girl go outside? That's horrid."

"I know. But it's complicated. She loves Cobie."

He isn't convinced. "Control is what she loves."

It's true, I know. But she isn't as bad as he makes her sound. She takes care of Cobie too.

"And you haven't told anyone? Not even Mother?"

"I promised I wouldn't. That's why she lets me visit. She doesn't even care about my cleaning. I just visit with Cobie. That's why she pays me."

"Ah." He nods his head dramatically. I know what he's thinking. That she'd *never* pay me for my cleaning abilities. Rude.

"How much do you have there?"

"Eighty guilders."

"*Eighty?*"

"It's a lot. I know."

"That's enough for a person to travel all the way to America."

"What do you mean?"

"I've been asking around. With ship fare, and food and supplies, it costs about eighty guilders to go to America. More like a hundred if you want to go beyond New York."

"I've been saving this so we *don't* have to go to America."

"Maybe you should reconsider."

I don't respond, but the truth is, I *have* been reconsidering.

He rises to go, but I stop him. "You have to promise not to tell anyone about this."

"Why should I?"

"Because I promised I wouldn't tell anyone."

"You just told me."

"The widow said if you found out I'd have to share it with you." I offer him thirty guilders.

He looks at the money. "To keep me quiet?"

"Exactly."

He shakes his head in disgust. "I don't want her money. I don't like the way she uses it."

"But you can't tell anyone."

"I won't. For your sake, not hers."

I still think he's being too hard on her. "It's her money. Why shouldn't she use it to get what she wants?"

"It isn't her money. Not really." He turns back to the ladder and starts to climb down. "Everything belongs to God. He gives us things to help people, not control them."

It's true, I know. But I don't tell him that. Nobody wants Theo thinking he's a doctor of philosophy or something.

After he's gone, I count the guilders again, just to be sure. Eighty. If I continue to earn ten guilders each week, I'll have five hundred guilders in a year. That will be enough for a family of five to go to America.

At dinner, Father wants to discuss plans for Sunday. We'll travel to Wittemeer for the morning service, have dinner with the Meers, then return home in time to help the Kosters set up their store for the evening service in Otten.

Theo says, "A friend of mine is planning to come to church with us. Anders de Haan."

Father's face lights up. "That's great news."

I'm happy for Theo. Anders is nice. Too bad he doesn't have any sisters.

"I think more will come," Father says. "Dirk seemed interested."

Dirk Holleman. No daughters.

"Miriam wanted to come last time," Mother says, "but her baby was sick."

Miriam Zager. Three daughters. All under the age of five.

I finally work up the courage to speak. "The widow Wolters needs me on Sunday morning."

Father looks at me. "On Sunday?"

"Just in the morning."

"What about church? We're going to Wittemeer."

"I know, but...she needs my help."

Mother looks doubtful. "Your help with what?"

I've been dreading this moment. If they knew about Cobie, they'd let me help. They'd insist I help. Even on Sunday. But they don't know. And I can't tell them.

"Well?"

"She hurt her foot." Not true, I know. But *Cobie* hurt her foot, so it's almost true. And also a big fat lie.

Father looks concerned. "How badly?"

"She stepped on some broken glass. The doctor says it's healing, but she still has a limp."

"Maybe I'll stop and see her tomorrow."

"No!" It comes out louder than I intended. I try to regain my composure. "She doesn't like people to know. She asked me not to say anything." Now I'm telling lie upon lie. It's actually getting easier.

Theo gives me a look. The one that says, "What are you up to?"

Mother still looks doubtful. "Why Sunday? You know we have church. *She* knows we have church."

"She said it has to be Sunday. Maybe she wants to go to church." That's the biggest lie yet. But it's the only story, other than the truth, that makes sense.

Father looks at Mother. "Why doesn't her brother help her?"

I didn't count on them knowing she has a brother. "He...I don't think they get along very well."

"I'm sure they don't. But he's an elder. He should want to help her get to church."

I open my mouth to respond, but nothing comes out.

Mother gives Father a look. The one that says, "She's your daughter. You deal with her."

I offer my strongest argument. It comes from the Bible. "We're supposed to lay down our life for our friends. That's what Rev. Hoek says. Like the good Samaritan. Like Jesus."

Father frowns. "But on Sunday?"

He's about to say no when Theo jumps in. "There is that thing about an ox in a ditch."

Father looks at him. "What?"

"Jesus said a farmer may help his ox out of a ditch. Even on Sunday."

Yes, Theo! I turn to Father. "Isn't the widow more important than an ox?"

He hesitates. "She's really hurt?"

I hesitate, then nod. "The doctor says she has to soak her foot every night. And put ointment on it."

He sighs, looks at Mother, then sighs again. "Alright, just this once."

CHAPTER TWENTY-FOUR

Sunday morning, I wake early, eat breakfast with my family, and go outside.

Father is hitching Samson to the wagon. He says, "Are you sure you'll be alright?"

"I'm sure."

Mother emerges from the house with a picnic basket to share with the Meers at dinner. She gives me a hug. "Promise you'll be careful."

"I promise."

"And come straight home after."

"I will."

"There's ham and cheese for your dinner. And you may have some applesauce."

"Thank you."

Theo helps Luc into the wagon and climbs up beside him. They all wave goodbye, and Father urges Samson into the lane.

As the wagon disappears into the distance, I question my decision to stay behind. It's true what Theo said about the ox and the ditch, but I still feel guilty skipping church. And for lying.

And what about my friends? Annika and Betsie will leave for America soon, and I'm giving up a chance to spend time with them. For what?

I know the answer. For Cobie.

The house feels eerily quiet. Like someone is watching me. I stand up and walk around the house. Nothing.

I have some time before I need to head to town. I wish I had my Bible storybook, but it's still in the widow's dustbin. I bring out our family Bible and it opens to Psalm 119. Verse 114 says, "Thou art my hiding place and my shield: I hope in thy word." It seems like that verse was written just for me. Sometimes I want to run away. Then God is my hiding place. Other times I want to stand and fight. Then God is my shield. Either way, he is protecting me.

When the time comes, I set out for Otten, timing my trip to arrive at the Brugplatz at half past nine. Clouds hang low, turning everything gray. In the distance a woodpecker sounds, tap, tap, tap.

The widow is waiting for me at the door. "Come in. We need to talk."

"We made a bargain."

"Yes, yes, but listen, I want to propose an amendment."

"What's that?"

"A change. Hear me out. I'll pay you more. I know you need money. Give up this idea of taking Cobie outside, and I'll double your pay."

I start to object, then stop. Double my pay!

Fear shows in her eyes, and I realize just how much she depends on my silence. How far will she go to protect her secret? This must be what power feels like.

Before I can say anything, I notice Cobie. She has fear in her eyes too—fear I'll go back on my word. I give the widow my answer. "No amendments."

"I'll give you twenty-five guilders per week."

I turn to Cobie. "Are you ready?"

A grin spreads across her face. "Ready."

The widow glares at me, but she won't go back on her bargain. She says, "Promise me you'll be back by quarter to eleven."

"We promise."

"If you see anyone, walk the other way."

"We will."

"If anyone asks about Cobie, tell them she's a distant cousin who came to stay with you for a few days."

I lead Cobie out into the street.

"Look!" Cobie crosses over to the patch of grass visible from her window. She bends down and runs her fingers through it. "It isn't prickly at all."

"Not now. It still has dew on it."

Cobie lays down in the grass. "It smells good."

We both laugh. A bird chirps, and Cobie points. "Did you hear that?"

Soon there are other sounds, each one bringing questions from Cobie. Then it's smells. "I didn't know each flower had its own smell."

I'm certain now that we're doing the right thing.

"Show me your favorite things," Cobie says. "Show me your church."

I had hoped to avoid the area around the church, but Cobie insists. And it is the prettiest building in town. She deserves to see it.

Her eyes go wide at the sight of the church. "Look at those windows."

"When you're inside, the light streams through the colored panes."

"Can we go in?" She starts up the steps.

"No!" I pull her back. "We can't let anyone see us."

The sound of singing spills into the street. I recognize the tune. It's Psalm 95. About how beautiful it is to worship in God's house. And here I am skipping church.

Cobie slips beneath an open window, letting the music wash over her.

My heart is pounding. We're too close. What if someone sees us? I have to get Cobie away.

The clock chimes ten o'clock and I jump at the opportunity. "Let's go see the clock tower."

We make our way to the town hall and admire the big clock. Next we walk to the market square. I show Cobie where we set up our booth to sell cheese.

Where we used to set up our booth. When we used to sell cheese. It's been nearly a month since we last worked the market, but the memory of that day still casts a shadow over my day.

I turn to Cobie. "What else would you like to see?"

"Sheep."

I laugh. "No sheep in town. Not on Sunday. But there are usually ducks on the canal." We walk to the White Bridge. Sure enough, several ducks swim in the quiet water below. They have shimmering green heads and bright yellow beaks.

The clouds are dark and lowering. I wish the sun would come out, so Cobie could enjoy the full beauty of the outdoors.

She wants to get closer to the ducks. She ignores my warnings and scrambles down to the water's edge. "They're so pretty. Just like a picture in a book."

The clock strikes half past ten. I suggest we turn back.

"Wait. Look!" Cobie points to a swan floating in the distance. She scrambles further down the bank to get a closer look.

We admire the cob's long arching neck. But it's getting late. I remind Cobie that we promised to be back by quarter to eleven. "Your aunt won't be happy if we're late."

Back on the High Street, we hurry toward the Brugplatz. Halfway there, Cobie falls to the ground and cries out in pain.

I turn to look. "What's wrong?"

"I twisted my ankle. These cobblestones are awful."

"Can you stand up?"

She tries but crumples back to the street. "It hurts."

My heart starts to pound again. Taking Cobie out is more work than I expected. Maybe this was a bad idea.

She looks up at me, on the verge of tears. "I'm sorry to be so much trouble."

"It's alright. But we have to get you home. Here. Put your arm around my waist."

With my help, she manages to stand. Tears come to her eyes, but she doesn't complain. The clock strikes quarter to eleven. She gives me a frightened look.

"Don't worry," I say. "We're almost there."

As we approach the Brugplatz, the street fills with older boys. They're laughing and shoving each other and having a great time. In the center of the group walks a boy with untamed yellow curls. Xander Bloem. He stops when he sees me. "Tess! What are you doing in town? And who's your friend?"

"I...we..." Maybe it's best not to answer.

"Did you have church this morning?"

No answer.

"Are you having church this evening?"

No answer.

He grins. "You're right. Sorry. None of my business."

I keep my arm around Cobie and continue walking.

He follows us.

We're at the Brugplatz, but I can't let him know we're heading to the widow Wolters' apartment, so I pretend to continue on.

Cobie tries to stop. "This is..."

"Shh."

"But Aunt..."

"Shh!"

"Who's your friend?" Xander asks again.

No answer.

He turns to Cobie. "You hurt your foot. I can help."

I step between them. "No. You can't."

He grins and flexes his muscles. "I can carry her wherever you want."

"No, thank you."

Another boy steps forward. Max Everhart. Eva's older brother. He grins, but his eyes are full of menace. "We can carry them both." He looks at Xander. "They're scolds, you know. We can carry them to the canal and dump them in."

Cobie's eyes go wide with fright. She puts her lips to my ear. "I don't swim."

Others press forward, but Xander holds them back with one arm. "I've got a better idea. Last one to Harmen's orchard has to pick peaches for the rest of us!" He takes off at top speed. The other boys race after him, laughing and shouting accusations. Max lingers a moment, scowling at me, then lumbers after them.

With the street empty, I breathe a sigh of relief.

"Who were they?" asks Cobie.

"Just boys from school."

"Who was the nice one?"

"There were no nice ones."

"The one who..."

"Never mind him. We need to get you inside."

The clock strikes eleven as we arrive at the widow's door. She herds us inside. "You're late."

"We were...delayed."

"I saw. What did you tell them?"

"Nothing."

"Good." She looks at Cobie. "Why are you limping?"

"I fell. But Tess helped me. Everything smells so good outside. Did you know each flower has its own smell?"

The widow ignores her comment. "That was a terrible risk."

"We saw the canal. It smells...watery. It sounds like it's laughing."

The widow isn't impressed. "I was frightened half out of my mind."

Cobie hobbles to her day bed and climbs in with a contented sigh.

I turn to go, but the widow stops me. "Wait. The streets will be full of people heading home from church. It'll be quiet again in half an hour." She motions to a chair. "I still can't believe your parents let you skip church." Her eyes hold something like admiration. "What did you tell them?"

I hang my head. "I had to make something up."

"Oh?"

"They might have gotten the idea that you...possibly...wanted to go to church."

"Me?" She chuckles. "When I was a girl, lying was a sin."

I hate that glint of humor in her eye. It's her fault I had to lie. "You won't let me tell the truth."

"Not about Cobie." She settles into a deep cushioned chair. "Not that."

We sit in silence. Finally, she says, "Tell me about your family. Your father works for Mr. Borgman."

I stare at her.

"You think I don't know things, but I do," she says. "Does your father enjoy his work?"

"He likes it fine." I can see she doesn't believe me. "Theo thinks Mr. Borgman is mean."

She chuckles. "Your brother is smarter than I gave him credit for. I went to school with witless Wendell Borgman. He was a bully then, and he hasn't improved with age. Your father should have stood up to him years ago."

"He would have lost."

"Is he winning now?"

We lapse into silence, then she says, "I knew your grandmother when we were young."

I look at her, surprised.

"We were friends. We had some fine adventures together."

I close my eyes and listen as she tells me stories of two girls pick-
ing apples together and boating on the canal. Then she sighs. "But
she married a local boy—Philip. He had no money. She knew that and
married him anyway. Later, my Simon came along. He was eight years
older than me. Established in business. Successful. Theresa and I lived
in different worlds."

She pauses. "Simon was a good man. Not without faults, mind
you. Stubborn as a mule, but a good man. We lived by the canal. I
loved that house. High ceilings. Lots of light. We were happy."

She gazes out the window, but her mind is far away in the past.
"My husband's business took him to the Hague. He met the king. He
was in line for a government position. Then he became ill. Cholera.
Six weeks later, he was gone."

"I'm sorry."

"Me too."

The clock strikes noon, and the widow stands up, scanning the
empty street. "People are settling down to their noon meal. Time for
you to go."

"Wait," Cobie says. "I have something before she leaves." She
hands me a package. "For your birthday." The paper is expensive but
clumsily wrapped.

"May I open it?"

"No! You mustn't open it until later."

"Thank you."

The widow holds out a fistful of guilders. "For spending the morning with Cobie."

"I can't accept that."

"Oh? Your finances have improved that much?"

"No." I look away. "People still won't buy our cheese. Mr. Jonkeer
won't allow it."

"Ah, Mr. Jonkeer." She holds out the guilders again. "Take them."

"I mustn't work on Sunday."

"Nonetheless, here you are."

"This isn't work."

"No? What is it then?"

"Charity, I guess. Love."

"Love?" She huffs. "You love Cobie, now?"

"Of course. And you."

"Me?" She turns away in disgust. "Don't waste your love on me."

CHAPTER TWENTY-FIVE

As soon as I'm out of sight of the widow's apartment, I unwrap Cobie's present. It's my own Bible storybook. The one the widow threw in the dustbin. Cobie rescued it, just like she promised.

Back at home, I eat the dinner Mother prepared for me. The ham is delicious, but I feel uneasy in an empty house.

Then I hear a noise. *Thump.*

No one else is home. I walk through the house. Nothing. Maybe I imagined it.

But there it is again. *Thump.*

It came from outside. I feel suddenly cold. Did someone in town see me? Did they guess I'm here alone?

From the window, I look out at the yard. Nothing. At least nothing I can see. I cross to the kitchen window. The yard is empty, but the door to the barn is open. Only six inches, but it's open. I'm certain it was closed before. At least I think I'm certain.

What if it's someone from the state church, thinking to harm Madam Maas while Father is away in Wittemeer?

What should I do? Scream? Hide? Run to one of our neighbors for help? I pick up a rolling pin, open the door, and cross the yard on my tiptoes.

This is silly, but my heart is racing. Maybe I dreamed the whole thing up. Maybe Father forgot to close the door in his haste to get to Wittemeer.

I'm at the barn door, about to turn back for the house, when I hear it again—an indistinct *thump* from inside the barn.

Suddenly the door swings open, and a figure bursts through it.

I scream and swing the rolling pin. *Thunk.*

"Aagh!" The intruder lets out a startled cry.

I wind up for another swing but stop when I recognize his face. Mr. Huizen!

"Tess! What are you doing here?"

I drop my weapon. "What are *you* doing here?"

"I'm seeing to the animals while your family is in Wittemeer."

Of course. How could he know I stayed behind?

He's still staring at me. "Why are you here?"

I can't answer. Not truthfully. So I change the subject. "I'm sorry I hit you. Did it hurt?"

He rubs his shoulder and grins. "Yes, actually."

"Please don't tell my parents I hit you."

"I won't. If you don't tell my wife I jumped and screamed like a child."

By midafternoon, my family returns from Wittemeer. They gather in the kitchen, eager to talk about their morning. They met at Mr. Waal's farm again. But a threat of rain moved their service into his barn.

"With cows!" Theo grins. Like that's a good thing.

"It was very clean," Mother assures me.

Theo plugs his nose and grins.

Luc plugs his nose too, and they both burst out laughing.

Mother says, "Annika and Betsie were sorry to miss you."

I'm sorry I missed them too.

Finally, Father asks the question I've been dreading. "How did *your* morning go?"

I don't have a good answer. All I can say is, "Good."

"Good?"

"I still think it's odd," Mother says.

"I still think *she's* odd," Theo says.

Father wants details. "What was the great emergency?"

"There *was* a good reason, but...she doesn't want me to say."

His eyes narrow. "I *do* want you to say."

"Can we talk about it later?"

"Oh, trust me. We will." He turns to Mother. "I'm going to speak to Jamus about this."

I look at Mother. "Who's Jamus?"

"Mr. Jonkeer. Her brother."

"Mr. Jonkeer is the widow's brother?"

"Of course," Mother says. "I thought you knew. She was a Jonkeer before she married."

I didn't know. How could I? That means the widow is...Julia's aunt!

They go back to talking about their morning in Wittemeer, but I don't even listen. How many times have I complained to the widow about Mr. Jonkeer? And all this time, he's her brother.

When we set out for Otten for the evening service, everyone seems tense. Are they afraid little Louis Jonkeer will meet us in the street with a handful of manure? I am.

Thankfully, Mr. Koster's store is five blocks from the state church. Even after we cross into town, we see few people.

At the store, Mr. Koster ushers us into his warehouse. The room is filled with benches and chairs, crates and barrels, anything a person can sit on, all facing a long table that holds a sort of pulpit.

The room smells of tobacco and coffee. It's warm but dimly lit, with only a row of windows near the ceiling to let in fresh air and sunlight.

The Vissers are here. And the Van Tils. Dirk Holleman and his family have taken seats near the front. Theo makes his way to the tallest barrel and hoists himself up, grinning like he's king of the world.

Uncle Ed and Betsie arrive, and with them, Rev. Hoek and the Meers.

Father welcomes them with a handshake. I welcome them too. "Betsie! Annika!"

We embrace, all talking at once.

"I'm so glad you made it."

"We had to, after you couldn't come this morning."

"We heard you had to help a widow."

"How fun!"

"It *was* fun. But I missed you."

"And here we are!"

We all laugh and hug again.

Mother gives us a look. The one that says, "Quiet down. We're in church."

We find a bench near the door and wait to see who else will come.

The Zagers arrive with their three small girls. Next come the de Haans. Theo waves for Anders to join him. Anders rolls a barrel closer to Theo and climbs aboard.

Annika smiles. "What is it about boys and barrels?" We all laugh.

A few more people arrive. More than last week but still only a few.

No Julia. No Nellie. None of my friends from town. But I didn't really expect them. I'm content with Betsie and Annika.

Rev. Hoek makes his way to the pulpit. He opens with prayer, and we sing Psalm 123. One of my favorites! He preaches from Hebrews 11, about being pilgrims and strangers in the earth. He says that all through history, God's people have suffered opposition. They've been afflicted, tormented, and imprisoned, forced to wander in deserts and mountains, to hide in dens and caves of the earth.

A shiver runs down my back. Could those things happen today?

He says that despite opposition, God always preserves his church. He never forsakes us. He reads Psalm 9:9, "The LORD also will be a refuge for the oppressed, a refuge in times of trouble."

Well into his sermon, a clamor rises from the street outside, as if people are shouting. The windows are set too high in the wall to see what's happening.

Rev. Hoek ignores the noise and continues to preach.

Using a long pole with a hook on the end, Mr. Koster closes the windows. That quiets the noise but makes the room even stuffier.

Rev. Hoek pauses from his preaching to wipe his forehead with a handkerchief.

Betsie fans herself with her songbook. My dress clings to my legs.

Rev. Hoek begins again. "When we find ourselves in times of trouble, we look about us for someplace where we can run. Someplace safe. As believers, we look to God. He is our refuge. He is—"

A sudden crash shatters the quiet. Shards of glass rain down from the window above.

People scream and scramble for cover. Mother leans over Luc, shielding him, but he still ends up with bits of glass in his hair.

Everyone is talking at once. Children are crying. Those seated under the windows scramble to get to the other side of the room.

One of the windows above has a gaping hole in it. Jagged angles of glass cling to the frame. On the floor lies a rock the size of my fist.

From outside, shouts and jeering come through the broken window.

Then another crash. Another broken window. The shouts grow louder.

Father and Uncle Ed rush to the door and out into the street.

I rise to follow, but Mother says, "Sit down." I sit but keep my eyes on the door. What's happening out there? I picture Louis Jonkeer readying a handful of manure.

Rev. Hoek suggests we sing Psalm 46, "God is our refuge and our strength, a very present help in trouble."

Halfway through the psalm, Father and Uncle Ed return. They approach the pulpit and speak to Rev. Hoek.

When the psalm ends, Rev. Hoek announces, "It seems a number of unruly youths are waiting outside, intent on causing trouble."

Mr. Koster stands up. "We have as much right to meet as the state church. We can't let them intimidate us."

Uncle Ed agrees. "I say we cause *them* some trouble."

Father says, "They're just boys. If we have something to say, let's take that up with the authorities tomorrow."

Rev. Hoek says, "Jesus faced opposition, and so must we. Let's face it as he did—with meekness. Repay evil with good. I'll close with prayer, then let's return to our homes."

Some grumble, but everyone returns to their seats. Rev. Hoek closes with prayer and dismisses us.

Mother orders me to remain near, but I manage to get to the door where I can see outside. It's mostly older boys, maybe forty of them. They bang on pots and pans and anything that makes noise. I know most of them from school. Max Everhart is there. He starts some of the boys singing a song with vulgar lyrics.

I feel ashamed that Annika has to hear it. I turn to her. "I'm so sorry."

"It's no better at home," Annika says. "We had to worship in a barn this morning."

"I know, but this is so..." I stop. There are no words for what this is.

Members of our small congregation enter the street and move off toward their homes. The boys in the street split up, following them and harassing them as they go.

Max Everhart leads one group. They follow the Zagers, pelting them with pebbles and trying to outdo each other with insults.

I spot Eva Everhart, watching from a nearby doorstep. She doesn't join in, but she doesn't try to stop them, either.

Mr. Zager keeps his head down and says nothing. I don't understand. He's a grown man. Why should he let sixteen-year-old boys treat him like that?

The street is churning with people. I spot Mr. Meers and Annika moving away down the street and hurry to join them.

Maarten Borgman and his friends follow us, shouting insults. It makes me so angry! Someone needs to stand up to Maarten, or he'll turn out just like his father.

He tries to push Mr. Meers, but Annika is in his way. He knocks her to the ground.

Theo helps Annika to her feet, then turns to face Maarten. "What are you doing? These people are just trying to go home. You push a girl?"

Some of the boys look guilty and embarrassed, like they don't really want to be there. But Maarten stands defiant. "You telling me what to do? Nobody tells me what to do."

"Theo!" Father takes his arm and pulls him away from Maarten. "Stick with us. We've got to get Rev. Hoek and the Meers back to their wagon."

Betsie and I stick close and sneak in one more hug with Annika before she climbs into her father's wagon and rolls back toward Wittemeer.

"What now?" Theo asks.

Father sighs. "We find Uncle Ed."

Back at Mr. Koster's store, Uncle Ed is in the street, red-faced from arguing with the boys who remain.

"Ed," Father says. "We're going home."

Uncle Ed has more to say. "Vandals! That's all you are!" With that he joins us as we make our way back toward the canal.

A handful of boys, led by Max Everhart, follow behind, calling us names. "Swine! Scolds!" Most of the boys stop when they reach the canal, but Max continues onto the bridge.

On the far bank, Theo stops. He turns around to face Max. Father doesn't notice.

Max does notice and stops abruptly. He's bigger than Theo, but soft around the middle, while Theo has muscles from years of work in the fields. Max glances to his left and right but finds himself alone on the bridge.

Theo takes a step toward Max and Max's eyes go wide with alarm. He steps forward, then back, like he can't make up his mind. Finally, he turns on his heel and saunters back to his friends, trying hard to pretend that was his plan all along.

Theo watches him go, then rejoins us.

When we're fifty yards distant, Max shouts, "We'll teach you what happens to scolds!"

CHAPTER TWENTY-SIX

On the walk back home, Uncle Ed fumes about the boys in town. "It's a disgrace. They should be locked up."

Theo tries to defend them. "Most of them aren't really bad. It's mostly just Max and Maarten."

Uncle Ed turns his anger on Theo. "They threw rocks through Mr. Koster's windows. That's a criminal offense."

Theo falls silent. Uncle Ed doesn't. "I'll tell you what's worse—the authorities knew about it and didn't try to stop it. They *let* it happen."

More silence. More Uncle Ed. "And how did they know where we were meeting? Are they spying on us now?"

"Let's not make more of this than it is," Father says. "We invited people to join us. Word was sure to get around."

That seems to calm Uncle Ed down. He says, "I invited Philip Bakker. He wasn't very happy about it. He probably went straight to the authorities."

Betsie motions to me, and we fall behind the others so we can talk. She says, "I was thinking, maybe you could stay overnight at my house tonight. I don't know how many more opportunities we'll have."

We catch back up to the others and she asks Uncle Ed, "Can Tess stay overnight at our house?"

"That's a good idea," he says. "You should be together tonight."

I ask Mother, "Can I?"

She nods. "As long as you come home in the morning and do your chores."

A night at Betsie's house is usually fun. Uncle Ed can be stern about church things, and I'm still upset he's taking Betsie to America, but he's not a stickler about bedtime.

When we arrive at their house, Betsie and I change out of our Sunday clothes and into her everyday clothes. They're a little tight on me, but I don't want to risk ruining my new dress.

Dusk settles over the fields as Uncle Ed prepares a plate of herring and a pot of pea soup. After supper, he gathers up the dishes and Betsie and I go outside to talk.

I can't stop thinking about what happened at church. They talk about love, then throw rocks through our windows. I say, "Tonight was horrid."

Betsie smiles. "The herring or the soup?"

I try not to laugh. "You know what I mean. Why do boys have to be so difficult?"

"It comes naturally to them. Like scratching their bellies and belching."

This time, I do laugh.

We lie down in a patch of tall grass, gazing up at the night sky. It's a cool night, the first cool night, the kind that signals that summer is coming to an end.

Betsie says, "Father thinks we'll leave for America before school starts."

A chill runs through me. Always before, I've looked forward to the start of school. I get to see my friends every day, play shuffleboard, and run races. But things will be different this year. The boys will probably call me names. The girls too. Maybe even my friends. Or will they refuse to talk to me? That would be worse. I know what to expect from Eva. But what about Julia? Are we still friends? And now I won't have Betsie.

A shooting star pierces the night. Betsie grabs my arm. "Did you see that?"

"I did!"

We scan the sky, hoping to see another. Two minutes later, a quick one skims just above the tree line. Ten minutes later, an especially bright one burns almost from horizon to horizon.

We lie side by side, hoping to see more stars shoot across the dark canvas of the sky. I say, "Do you think those were angels?"

She looks at me. "No."

"It's just...the Bible says that stars sang at the time of creation, and I heard once, that meant angels."

She considers that. "I guess I've heard that too."

"So maybe they *were* angels."

"I don't think so." She shakes her head. "Angels are angels, and stars are stars."

"I suppose. But I think about angels when I see stars. Like they're watching over me."

She considers that for a moment. "Do you think they have shooting stars in America?"

"Of course. Are you getting excited to go?"

"Not without you."

"Annika will be there."

"I know, but you'll be here. All alone."

"I won't be alone."

She snort-laughs. "You'll always have Eva."

After a moment, I say, "Can I tell you a secret?"

She turns to face me. "You must."

"I've been saving some money. At first, I thought it would help my family stay in the Netherlands. Now, I think it might be better to go to America." I didn't intend to admit that to anyone, but now that I've said it, it sounds right.

She says, "Really? I hope you do."

"Not right away. It will probably take another year."

"That's not so long. How are you able to save money when people won't buy your cheese?"

"It's a long story."

"We have all night."

I want to tell her about the widow. About Cobie. But I can't.

And Father shows no sign of changing his mind. But if he ever does, I'll be ready. I imagine how it might happen. One day Father will realize we have no choice but to leave the Netherlands and go to America. But how? We have no money. In our darkest hour, I will hand him a burlap sack filled with guilders and ask, "Is five hundred enough?"

Suddenly, Betsie grabs my hand. I hear it too. Voices. Not from the lane but from the trees, just a few dozen paces away. They're louder now.

Footsteps crunch in dry grass. A voice says, "Be quiet."

Another says, "I *am* being quiet."

They sound like boys. Older boys. And they aren't being quiet.

"What if we get caught?"

"We won't get caught. And besides, it's no big deal. We're just going to scare him."

"How?"

"You'll see."

"I don't want to get caught."

"We won't get caught. And even if we do, no one will care. He's a scold. He's the *chief* scold."

"I heard he's already planning to leave."

"Yeah. I heard that too."

"So why do we have to scare him?"

"Don't be a baby. Follow me." A group of shadowy figures step out from the trees and cross the yard toward Uncle Ed's barn.

When it's safe, I whisper, "We should follow them."

Betsie shakes her head. "I have to tell my father."

The figures enter the barn, and we sprint for the house.

"This way." Betsie leads me around to the back door and slips inside. The house is quiet. Uncle Ed is nowhere to be seen.

Betsie knocks on his bedroom door. "Are you awake?"

"Yes."

"Someone's outside. They went in the barn."

He opens the door. His nightshirt hangs down to his knees. "Who?"

"I don't know. We heard them talking. They want to scare us."

He lights a lantern. "Stay here. I'll go have a look." He gathers a spade from the garden and strides out toward the barn.

Betsie and I follow. Uncle Ed's horse stamps and snorts inside the barn.

Uncle Ed stops. He turns to us. "Go back to the house."

We start to obey, but when he turns back to the barn, so do we.

At the door, Uncle Ed stops. "Who's in there? What do you want?"

A shuffling sound, but no answer.

He pulls the door open. His lantern casts a dim circle of light, not enough to illuminate every corner of the barn, but enough to see his horse, stamping and blowing through its nostrils.

He enters the barn.

We follow.

He rubs his hand down the big horse's neck. "It's alright, boy." He walks up to his wagon and peers over the edge to see if anyone is hiding inside.

Off to my left, something moves. A voice shouts, "Run!" and the barn explodes with motion.

I scream as a whirl of dark shapes rush past. One of them collides with Betsie, knocking her to the ground.

"Hey!" Uncle Ed pursues them outside. "What's this all about?"

I emerge from the barn in time to see six figures fleeing into the cover of the trees. With shock, I realize two of them are girls. One runs like Eva, with long ungainly strides. The other is quick and compact, with long dark curls streaming behind her.

Betsie brushes herself off and joins me. "Who was it?"

"I don't know." I'm fairly certain the tall girl was Eva. But the other one, well, lots of girls have dark curls. And even blond hair can look dark at night.

Uncle Ed shouts after them. "I know who you are. The authorities will hear about this." He drops his spade and chases after them. He stops at the edge of the woods, and I race past him. Low-hanging branches claw at my clothing. I keep running, using my arms to shield my face.

"Tess!" he cries. "Stop!"

I stop, surrounded by dark trees. I listen for voices. Nothing. Silence. Have they outrun me? Or are they hiding in the trees, just footsteps away?

Uncle Ed appears with his lantern, breathing hard.

"I can catch them," I say. "I'm a good runner."

He leans over, catching his breath. "I can't have you running off alone."

Betsie joins us, still brushing straw from her clothes. "What were they up to?"

Uncle Ed scowls after them. "Nothing good."

"Who were they?" she asks. "You said you knew."

Even in the darkness, I can see the frustration in his eyes. "I don't know, but I have my suspicions."

"Mr. Everhart? Mr. Jonkeer?"

He shakes his head. "No. Younger."

I agree. They didn't run like old men.

"Who, then?"

"Those same boys who interrupted church tonight."

That's likely. But they weren't just boys.

We return to the barn and check on Uncle Ed's horse. He's still restless. Uncle Ed strokes his neck, then walks over to where the intruders were gathered. His lantern reveals several palm-sized rocks scattered on the ground. They're the same size as the ones that came through the windows at church.

He pushes those rocks aside and picks up another, smaller one. He holds it to the light.

I've seen rocks like that before—flat and dark, with sharp edges. It's flint. Theo has one he uses sometimes to start fires.

Uncle Ed's eyes are still fuming, but he looks suddenly nervous. He glances at me. "We should warn your family."

With a start, I realize he's right. If this group planned something horrid, some other group might do the same at my house.

I look at Betsie. "I have to go."

Uncle Ed offers to hitch up his wagon and give me a ride home, but I say, "No. You have to stay. They might come back. And I can get home faster on foot."

Before he can argue, I race off into the night.

CHAPTER TWENTY-SEVEN

I sprint to the far side of Uncle Ed's house and past his garden to the path that leads home. I know the way by heart. I've taken it a thousand times. But still, the darkness slows me down. And this is no time for a twisted ankle.

Beyond the garden, I skirt a wheat field and continue on to the pine grove. From there, I come to the canal. Moonlight trembles on the water. My mind races ahead. What will I find when I reach home? Broken windows? Or something worse? I pick up my pace.

When I finally clear the last row of trees and spot my house, relief washes over me. Everything seems peaceful. No broken windows. No sign of intruders. Warm lantern light glows in the window where Father does his Sunday evening reading.

I slow to a walk, trying to calm myself before approaching the house. I take in a deep breath of cool, evening air, but immediately stiffen. The air smells like...smoke.

But where is it coming from? Not from our chimney. And no one would start a burn pile on Sunday. Then it catches my eye. An orange glow reflecting on the trees behind the barn. It flickers just like..."Fire!"

At first, nothing happens. I'm not sure if I screamed out loud or just in my head. Then Father bursts through the door. He's followed by Theo. They both look at me like I'm a stranger. "What are you... Why are you hollering?"

"Fire!" I point to a slim column of smoke rising from behind the barn.

"That's not..." Father looks more puzzled than alarmed. Then the orange glow reappears, and he gasps. He rushes off toward the barn with Theo at his heels. I race to catch up.

"Tess!" Mother calls from the doorway. "Come inside!"

I pretend not to hear.

At the back of the barn, someone has built a pile of sticks and set it on fire. Flames from the sticks have spread to the lower planks of the barn. Father tears off his shirt. He uses it to beat at the flames, but they refuse to go out.

"Theo!" Father shouts. "Get the cows out of the barn. Tess, get Samson out."

Samson! He's trapped inside! Right now, the flames are limited to the back wall of the barn, but what if they spread? I race to the front of the barn and open the door.

As I pass the ladder to the loft, I remember the guilders I have hidden up there. I need to get them out of the barn. But first, Samson.

The air in the barn is warm and thick. Samson snorts and blows through his nostrils. I open his stall, urging him forward.

He stamps his feet, refusing to come out.

I try to guide him forward, but he turns his back on me. This would be easier if I had an apple to tempt him with.

Theo is busy moving cows out of their stalls. I call to him for help, but he doesn't hear. He's having trouble with Madam Maas, who refuses to cooperate.

I turn back to Samson. "Come on, boy." I slip in along his left side. He's trembling all over. His neck is wet with perspiration.

"Come on, Samson." I force myself in front of him and press my shoulder against his chest. He rises up on his hind legs, protesting, then comes down again, nearly knocking me to my knees. But he turns partway around.

Again, I lean into him. Again, he turns. Once more, and I have him facing the right way.

"Go." I nudge him toward the barn door. He isn't interested. He wants to stay in his stall. "Come on. Get moving." I slap him on his rump.

Finally, he lunges forward, bursting out into the night air. He turns once, and again, then gallops to the far side of the pasture.

I start after him but stop at the ladder. All my dreams are up there. This is my chance.

"Tess!" Theo has Madam Maas out of her stall and moving toward the door. "Get to the pump. We'll need water!"

Water! I grab a half dozen milking buckets from pegs on the wall and rush to the pump. I place the first bucket under the spigot and work the pump's long arm.

Water splashes into the bucket. Too slowly.

Finally, one bucket fills, then another.

Theo grabs both buckets and races off to the back of the barn, water sloshing from side to side as he goes.

I continue working the pump.

Luc appears at the kitchen window, his face smashed up against the glass. Mother emerges from the house, picks up two full buckets, and hurries off to join the others.

When Theo returns, his face and arms are dark with soot. I ask him, "What's happening?"

He trades buckets and rushes off again without answering.

I pump as fast as I can. By the eighth bucket, my arms ache. By the tenth, my shoulders scream. I feel like every pump will be my last. I switch arms. That brings relief, but only for a moment. By the twelfth bucket, I'm certain I can't go on.

From the back of the barn, a crash splits the night. Mother screams. A thousand sparks leap into the sky.

What happened? I stop pumping and race to see.

Father emerges from a cloud of smoke. "Something gave way! Theo's pinned inside." He plunges back into the barn.

Mother stands speechless, flames reflecting in her eyes.

I hesitate. What should I do?

A moment passes—it seems like an hour—and Father emerges again. He takes a deep breath and plunges back in.

This time, I follow him.

Inside the barn, the smoke seems to clear. Air rushes through, making a strange whooshing sound.

Theo is on his back, one leg pinned under a wooden post. Father drops to his knees, struggling to lift it. His feet keep slipping on loose straw that covers the wooden slats of the floor.

I spot an old basin in the corner, one that Mother once used to make cheese. I topple it and slide it toward Father.

He wedges the basin between himself and the wall. Bracing his legs against it, he puts his shoulder into the post. It moves, but only an inch. Theo grabs his leg with both hands and pulls. Pain twists across his face, but he manages to wrench his leg free.

Father helps him to his feet, and we stumble from the barn, sucking in the cool night air.

Theo groans and collapses to the ground, dragging himself away to a safe distance.

Another eruption sends sparks streaking across the night sky like shooting stars. I think of angels.

Mother kneels at Theo's side, checking his injured leg.

I pick up the empty buckets and look to Father. "Shall I draw more water?"

He shakes his head. "It's too late. It's too dangerous."

The flames cover the entire back wall of the barn now but haven't spread to the rest of the barn yet. My savings are still in there. I still have time.

"Look!" Theo points to embers drifting up and over the house. Some land on the cheese shed and flare up.

Father leaps into action. "We've got to wet the roof. Tess! More water."

I race to the pump. Father leans a ladder against the house. Mother brings him buckets of water, which he sloshes over the roof of the house and the cheese shed.

Sparks land on the moistened roof, sizzle briefly, and go out.

"It's working," Father cries. "Keep the water coming."

I pump as quickly as I can.

Theo limps over to join me at the pump. "Let me help."

"You're hurt."

"Just my leg. I can still pump." He takes the handle and works it in strong, steady motions. Water gushes into the waiting bucket.

I step aside, then turn to face the barn. Is there still time? I slip away in that direction, then duck inside.

The loft is filling with smoke, but the ladder is still visible. I grab hold and begin to climb.

Smoke fills my nostrils and stings my eyes as I climb. I make my way across the loft to the gap in the beams that holds my treasure. I can't see the beams through the smoke, but I know the way. I step forward, putting out my hand, reaching for the cross beam.

It isn't there. I take another step. Still no beam. Where is it? Have I gotten turned around? I'm getting confused.

Unsure where I am, I slide my feet forward. Flames flicker off to one side, turning the smoke orange and red.

The heat grows more intense. I want to tear off a strip of cloth to cover my face, but I'm still wearing Betsie's clothes. I can't tear those, so I simply gather some cloth up in one hand and hold it over my mouth and nose.

The smoke grows thicker. I feel lightheaded and worry I might faint. I drop to my hands and knees. Yes. That's better.

Crawling forward, I hope to bump into something familiar. *Anything* familiar. Instead, my one free hand comes down on open air. I must be at the edge of the loft. But which way to the ladder?

Suddenly, the room begins to spin. I try to scream but make no sound. Darkness closes around me.

CHAPTER TWENTY-EIGHT

"Tess! Wake up!" It's Theo's voice. I open my eyes. I'm outside, in the yard between the house and the barn.

He stands over me, a bucket of water in his hands.

"Don't!" I say.

He does. Ice-cold water splashes over my head and shoulders.

I sputter and choke, wiping water from my eyes.

He raises another bucket.

"Stop!"

He doesn't. More water.

"Enough!" I sit up.

Father and Mother kneel at my side. "Are you alright?"

"What happened?"

"You were in the barn!" Mother says. "What if Theo hadn't thought to look for you there? We would have lost you!" Her voice is verging on hysteria.

I look past her at the barn. The whole thing is in flames now. I try to stand, but Mother holds me down. "What were you doing in there?"

Theo gives me a warning look, but I'm too confused for caution. "I have money hidden in there."

Mother looks at me like I'm out of my right mind. "Money? *That* was worth risking your life for?"

I burst into tears. Not little silent tears. Big sobbing tears. How can I explain? The money isn't for fun and games. Or even food or drink. It's for freedom. For America, where we can worship God freely. Where Theo can farm his own land. Where Luc can attend a good Christian school. Sometimes earthly things and spiritual things get all tangled together.

For a long time, we sit and watch the flames. Then Father says, "Here's what I don't understand. How did it start? No one went near the barn this evening."

I wipe tears from my cheek. "I can tell you."

They all look at me. I explain what happened at Uncle Ed's house.

Theo isn't convinced. "I can't believe someone would do this on purpose."

I give him a look. "Don't be naïve."

He starts to say something, then stops. "What's naïve? I don't even know what that means."

I hesitate to explain. I didn't mean it as an insult. Maybe a little.

Mother says, "It means believing in others even when we should know better. At your age I'd rather you be naïve than cynical."

He doesn't say anything, but I can see it in his eyes. He doesn't know what cynical means either.

Flames escape through the roof of the barn, stabbing into the night. I blink back tears. Everything is lost. My savings, my dreams, my future, all gone.

I lie back on the grass and stare up at the sky. If there are stars up there, I can't see them. Clouds of smoke blot them out.

Monday, I wake to sunlight streaming through my window. I can't even remember going to sleep. I sit up with a start. The barn!

Where the barn once stood, there now lies a pile of smoking rubble. Most of the beams still stand, but the roof is gone. The walls have caved in.

Madam Maas and the other cows stand in the pasture, munching on grass as if nothing happened. Samson stands tethered to our old sycamore tree.

A soft breeze tickles the leaves. Birds flutter and sing. They almost convince me that life will go on. Then I spot Mr. Borgman's black carriage standing in the yard. Like a dark cloud.

Mr. Borgman walks the length of the barn, examining the wreckage and puffing his ridiculous pipe. Father follows at a respectful distance. When Mr. Borgman has seen enough, he turns and barks something at Father.

I'm too far away to hear what he says, but it isn't hard to imagine. His jowls quiver and his cheeks puff out red with anger. His words are as sharp as the finger he points at Father's chest.

Father says nothing.

I have no such self-control. I want to kick something. Someone. Father didn't do anything wrong. His quick thinking saved Samson and the cows. He risked his life trying to save the barn. He did save the house and the shed.

But Mr. Borgman doesn't care about that. With all his wealth and influence, all he can think to do is treat Father like an irresponsible child in need of a stern rebuke.

He marches Father over to his carriage, and together they ride off toward town.

I take the opportunity to search through the rubble of the barn. Maybe, by some miracle, a burlap sack full of ten-guilder notes survived the flames. I keep up the search for almost an hour. All I find are a rusted scythe blade and a couple of old horseshoes.

About to give up, I spot a clump of something in the corner, covered in ash. My heart stops. It's about the right size. I kneel down, clear away the ash, and discover...a shovel handle. Charred and black. Worthless. Nothing survived the heat and flames. There will be no miracles.

Theo hobbles over. "Find anything?"

"No."

He turns to go.

I say, "Wait. How's your leg?"

He shrugs.

"You should see Dr. Brink."

"He was here this morning. You were asleep."

"What did he say?"

"He left some ointment. I'll be fine."

Back in the house, Mother greets me with a smile, doing her best to look cheerful. I don't know how she does it.

"We're pilgrims and strangers," she says. "We look to a city whose builder and maker is God."

It's true, I know. But where will Samson and the cows sleep?

At suppertime, Father returns from town. On foot. Mother greets him at the door with a kiss.

We eat in silence, waiting for Father to say whatever it is he isn't saying.

Mother says, "The blackberries down by the lane are ripe. I was thinking of making a cobbler."

I just can't be like that. I ask him, "What did Mr. Borgman say?"

He picks up his napkin, then sets it down again. "Mr. Borgman said he greatly respects us. He is thankful for our labors all these years."

"And?"

"And...he can't afford any more risk to his property and investment."

"What does that mean?"

"It means he'll be looking for a new farm manager. We may stay through the end of the harvest. After that, I'll need to look for new employment."

Mother gasps. "What about the house?"

"We'll have to find a new one."

He's serious. Mr. Borgman is kicking us out of our house. The only home I've ever known.

Theo stands up, forgetting his bad leg, and winces in pain. "He can't do that. It isn't right."

"He can."

"What will we do?" I ask.

Father sighs. "I've already spoken to a number of people in town. Hopefully someone can use a competent farm manager."

Theo slumps back into his chair. "Until they burn down *his* barn."

"I'll find work. One way or another. What else can we do?"

"We could go to America," Theo says. "Like Uncle Ed."

Father nods. "I wish we could. I'll confess, I've let my love for this land blind me to what's best for my family. Freedom of worship. Christian education. Those things are important. If I had the money, we'd go. If I had a rich uncle to borrow from, we'd go. But we simply don't."

I want to scream. This is the moment I've waited for. The darkest hour. When I present Father with a stack of guilders. And save the day. But now the moment has come, and I have nothing to offer. No money. No hope. No future.

After supper, I go outside to think. There are no rich uncles. But there is someone. Someone with plenty of money. More than she needs.

How can I convince the widow to help us? She won't do it out of the goodness of her heart. She doesn't have that kind of heart.

Theo follows me outside. "What about your widow friend?"

"She's not my friend," I say, spinning around.

"She has money."

"So?"

"Maybe she'll help us."

"She won't."

"How do you know?"

"She doesn't believe in charity."

He smiles grimly. "I wasn't thinking of charity. She'll do anything to keep her secret. If you tell people what you know, she'll lose everything she thinks is important."

"I can't do that. I gave my word."

"You don't have to break your word. Just suggest you *might*. Unless she pays."

"Theo! That's devious."

"Yeah. I suppose. But that's what *she'd* do."

CHAPTER TWENTY-NINE

Tuesday morning, I wake to a gray, overcast sky. Father and Theo are already gone, probably in the fields, working to assure Mr. Borgman a good harvest.

I set out for Otten. The widow will be expecting me. Cobie too. I usually look forward to my time there, but not today. I dread what I have to do.

Once I reach town, I take a small detour. There's something I need to do first. I make my way to the Hoofdstraat, to Julia's house. The Jonkeers live in a neighborhood of large homes with plenty of trees. Their home is one of the nicest.

A maid opens the door. She's new. I haven't seen her before. She smiles and asks, "May I help you?"

"I'd like to see Julia."

"I'm afraid Julia isn't home today. She's at a friend's house."

"Do you know which friend?"

"I'm sorry. I don't remember her name."

"Anna!" Mrs. Jonkeer's voice calls from inside the house. "Come here."

"Just a moment," she replies. "We have a guest at the door."

"Who?"

"One of Julia's friends."

"Send her away."

She gives me an apologetic smile. "I'm sorry."

"Wait," I say. "Can you describe her friend?"

"Certainly. A tall, pale, unpleasant thing." She winks at me and closes the door before I can thank her.

The Everharts' home is even larger than the Jonkeers'. It's guarded by tall hedges and a bristling wrought iron fence.

I hear Eva and Julia before I see them. They're arguing.

"We need to find Tess." Julia's voice is urgent. "We need to talk to her."

Eva sounds bored. "I don't see why. We didn't do anything."

They both fall silent when I appear. Julia hesitates, then throws her arms around me. "I'm so sorry to hear about your barn."

"My father told us all about it," Eva says. "He knows everything that happens around Otten."

I turn to face her. "Does he know who set the fire?"

She backs up a step. "Well, no. Obviously not that."

"Can you think of anyone who would do something like that?"

She looks uncomfortable. "Probably lots of people *wanted* to. But that doesn't mean they did."

I turn to Julia. She won't even look at me.

It was a mistake to come here. It doesn't matter what they know or don't know. I turn and walk away.

Back on the High Street, I make my way toward the Brugplatz.

Footsteps sound on the street behind me. "Tess. Wait."

It's Julia. She's alone. She says, "I wanted to tell you…"

"Tell me what?"

"Eva's brother found out where you were worshiping. Betsie's father must have invited Mr. Bakker to your worship service. He told Mr. Everhart and Max overheard. Max talked the other boys into causing trouble."

"And who decided to burn down our barn?"

"I don't know. I really don't. Eva doesn't either."

"What about Betsie's house? Do you know anything about that?"

She opens her mouth, then closes it again.

"I suppose you were home in bed."

"No."

"What then?"

Her lip trembles. "What if...a person was there, but not to do anything bad, just..."

"Perfectly innocent, I suppose."

"Not innocent. No. But just going along...not realizing what might happen." She grasps my hand. "Isn't that possible?"

I say, "Sure, Julia, I believe you. Go back to Eva. She's waiting for you." Again, I turn and walk away. Is that horrid of me? I don't care. But here's the problem. I *do* believe her. Who's being naïve now?

At the widow's apartment, Cobie rushes to greet me. "Aunt Ruth told me about your barn."

The widow nods gravely. "It's unfortunate, but these things happen."

"It didn't just *happen*. Someone *made* it happen. Someone started the fire on purpose."

"I know," she says. "Those things happen too."

"And now Mr. Borgman is kicking us out of our house."

"I told you before, your father should have stood up to Mr. Borgman. If nothing else, it would have given him some satisfaction."

"He can't afford satisfaction. He has a family to feed. You don't know how difficult things are. People are struggling. Some are even leaving the Netherlands for America."

I say it to shock her. But she isn't shocked. "I read the papers. Good for them. I hope they find refuge there."

Something about the way she says "refuge" strikes me as wrong. America isn't our refuge. *God* is. We can't put our trust in earthly things.

But what if God protects his people by making it possible for them to go to America? Sometimes spiritual things and earthly things get all tangled together.

"I don't have plans this morning," the widow says. "You should go home. Be with your family."

It's a generous offer, but I can't go home. Not yet. "I need to ask a favor."

"Oh?"

"We—my family—we want to go to America too."

Cobie gasps. Her eyes go round with fright.

A smile flickers in the widow's eyes. "Don't let *me* stop you."

"We don't have the money."

Her smile spreads to her lips. "Then I guess you won't be going to America. It's too bad. Your father would do well there. He's just the kind of man who would."

It's true. Father *would* do well in America. Theo too. Even Mother. Her cheese business could flourish there. More importantly, we'd be free to worship God without fear of opposition.

The widow says, "You could go back to the state church."

"No." I shake my head. "We can't do that."

"It would solve your problem, though."

"No. We have to worship where God's word is taught. I know that now."

"Even if it leaves you homeless and hungry?"

"Even then."

"So what does any of this have to do with me?"

"You have money. You could help us." I let out a big breath. She might laugh at me. She might get angry. But at least I tried.

She doesn't laugh or get angry, but she does look irritated. "I hope you don't expect charity because your grandmother was my friend. She married a poor farmhand. I married a man of means. We made our choices. Don't look to me to solve your problems."

CHAPTER THIRTY

Out on the street, I turn toward home. I should be happy. The widow accepted my bargain. My family can go to America.

But the widow was right to have so many questions. Where *will* I live? Where will I go to church? How will I get to America? I'll never convince Father and Mother to go unless I have answers.

I stop at the Huizens' on the way home.

"Come in," Mrs. Huizen says. "Are you selling cheese? I don't see your cart."

"Not today. I have a favor to ask."

"Of course. Anything."

"It's a big one."

"What's on your mind?"

I tell her my situation.

Before I can even ask, she says, "You can stay with us." She seems excited at the possibility.

Mr. Huizen joins us from the other room. "You're welcome to live here, but are you sure your parents will want that?"

"I don't know," I say, turning to face him. "I wanted to check with you, first."

"They might not approve. We still go to the state church."

That's true, of course. But where else can I go? I tell him, "I have to figure some things out yet. Please don't tell them I said anything."

He smiles. "Your secret is safe with us."

Mrs. Huizen pats her belly. "We've been keeping a little secret, ourselves. It's getting harder to hide."

I stare at her and gasp.

They both laugh at me. "Yes," she says. "We're expecting a baby. Early next year."

"Congratulations."

"Thank you."

"And you'll still let me live here?"

"We'd love some help when the baby comes."

I leave the Huizens, half excited at their kindness and half convinced my parents will never allow it. I have one more stop to make before heading home.

It's afternoon when I return home. Theo is waiting for me when I enter the yard. "Did you talk to the widow?"

"Yes."

"What did she say?"

"She agreed to help us."

"Ha! You didn't think she would."

"It's not out of the goodness of her heart."

He looks at me, surprised. "You actually threatened to tell her secret? I didn't think you'd do it."

"I didn't. I couldn't."

"What then?"

"We made a bargain. A business arrangement."

His eyes narrow. "What did you agree to do?"

"She'll pay for passage to America. Ship's fare. Food supplies. All of it. Everything we need."

"On what condition?"

"I'm going to stay behind and help her. Just for a while."

"Here? In the Netherlands?"

"Until I can earn enough to pay her back."

"How long?"

"One year. Fourteen months."

"A whole year?"

"Fourteen months."

He shakes his head. "This isn't your problem to fix. You're only thirteen."

"I'm fourteen. By next year, I'll be fifteen."

"How will you travel? They don't let thirteen-year-olds—"

"Fifteen."

"—travel alone on oceangoing vessels."

I turn and walk away. It seems I still have questions that need answering.

At supper, Father says, "I have a possible job offer. It's in Bentham."

Mother looks up. "What kind of job?"

"Cutting peat."

She frowns. "That's such difficult work."

"It's temporary. Until I find something better."

"I can help with expenses," Theo says. "Remember? Mr. Jaeger offered me work in Amsterdam."

"We can all help," Mother says. "I can take in cleaning. Tess can find work in town."

Father shakes his head. "That's not what I want, Theo in Amsterdam, Tess in town, you so tired you don't have time for Luc."

I say, "There is another way."

They all look at me. Theo shakes his head, as if to say, "Don't do it."

But I have to. Careful not to mention Cobie, I explain about the widow and our bargain.

"What's bargain?" Luc asks.

"A business arrangement."

"What's a 'rangement?"

"That's easy," Theo says. "It's when the widow gets her way, no matter who she has to hurt."

"That's not true," I argue. "It was my idea."

Mother frowns. "She has no business getting your hopes up. She doesn't have that kind of money."

"She does," I insist.

"It doesn't matter." Father is getting annoyed. "We're not going to America without you. How could she suggest such a thing?"

"It was my idea. It's only for a year..."

"Fourteen months," Theo says.

I glare at him and turn to Father. "It makes perfect sense. You can go now, find land, and begin to clear it. Theo can help. By spring, you'll be ready to plant. You don't need me for that. Then, next year, I'll come and join you."

"Where will you live in the meantime?" Mother asks.

"With the Huizens."

She sighs. "I know you like them, but we can't ask them to take on that kind of responsibility."

"They want to. They already told me."

Father raises an eyebrow. "You talked to them about this?"

"They said they'd be happy to have me stay with them."

"What about Sundays? They still go to the state church."

"The Kosters will pick me up for church on Sundays. They'll bring me to Wittemeer and back home again after."

"You talked to them too?"

"I did."

"All without saying a word to us?"

"Just today. On my way home from town."

Mother rolls her eyes. "Anything else you'd like to tell us?"

"Yes. Mrs. Huizen is expecting a baby."

Their eyes go wide with surprise, but they refuse to be distracted from the question at hand. Theo says, "We're not leaving without you."

I turn to Father. "It's the only way."

He isn't convinced. "I'll find work, and we'll save some money, and we'll find a way to go next year."

"But this way you can go right away."

"No." He puts a hand on my shoulder. "My answer is no."

CHAPTER THIRTY-ONE

Today is Wednesday, September 2, and I stand alone on the banks of the Rhine River in the great port city of Rotterdam. At the dock stands the *Princess Sophia*, a huge three-masted sailing ship about to set sail for America. Seagulls dip and dive in the salty breeze as I try to find my family, who have already gone onboard.

Let me bring you up to date. It's been three weeks since I made my bargain with the widow. That first day at home, Father completely rejected the idea. Three days later, we were still arguing about it. Theo argued most of all.

Then things began to change. First, Father wasn't able to find work as easily as he hoped. Wealthy landowners refused to meet with him. Those who did talk to him told him they wouldn't hire him because he'd chosen to worship in a free Reformed church.

Next, the Huizens stopped by and spoke with Mother. They convinced her they're more than willing to take me in. And the Kosters assured Father I could ride with them to Wittemeer each week for church. And Rev. Hoek promised to keep an eye out for trustworthy families who planned to travel to America. He was confident he could find a suitable family to serve as my escort next year.

The biggest change came when Father and Mother visited the widow Wolters. I don't know what she told them, but after that visit, they finally accepted the idea of my staying behind.

Theo took a bit longer. Every time the subject came up, he said, "I'll stay behind too. I can work for Mr. Jaeger in Amsterdam and check on Tess every weekend."

And every time, I said, "Father will need your help in America. He'll have to purchase land, clear it, turn it, plant crops, and tend them. He can't do that all by himself."

Once Father and Mother made the decision to go, everything happened quickly. The widow saw to all the details of the ocean passage. She bought tickets on the *Princess Sophia*, the same ship that Uncle Ed and Betsie will be traveling on, and provisions for up to six weeks at sea.

Mother made lists of what to take and what to leave behind. She insisted on bringing all of Grandmother's delftware, even though Father warned her they'd probably break into a thousand pieces by the time they reach America.

Mrs. Huizen showed me the room that will serve as my bedroom for the next year. It's more than large enough, with a window that looks out onto her flower garden. She's even letting me help decorate it. Did I mention that she's one of the nicest people ever?

I continued to visit Cobie and clean the widow Wolters' apartment. And I began tutoring Cobie in subjects I've learned in school. She's excellent at sums, but her spelling is horrid. She's happy I'm staying but sorry I can't go to America with my family. I guess I'm happy and sad too.

Last week, Julia came to see me at my house. I was helping Mother clean out the cheese shed when, all of a sudden, there she stood. Mother went to check on Luc so we could talk.

"I was just looking at your barn," she said, "or...what's left of it. It's so sad. I almost turned around and went home."

"I'm glad you didn't."

"I just wanted to tell you again that I didn't have anything to do with that."

"I know you didn't."

"I don't know who did."

"I believe you."

"Eva doesn't know either."

I didn't respond to that.

We walked out by the canal and talked about normal things—her new sister, Marianne, the cooler weather, my family's plans for America. We turned back when we reached the pines and ran all the way home. It wasn't a race, but just for fun.

Before she left, she said, "School starts soon. Will you be there?"

I nodded yes.

"Good," she said. "I'm glad."

Later, I wondered how school will be this year. It was nice to talk to Julia. But how will it be when Eva is there, working to drive a wedge between us? And no Betsie there to support me?

On Saturday, I saw Xander Bloem in town. He said, "I heard that your family is going to America."

"That's true."

"I might go to America someday."

"Really? Why?"

"Why not?" He grinned. "Truth is, I don't love the plans my father is making for me."

"What kind of plans?"

"Some school in Germany. He wants me to be a lawyer. Or a minister like him."

"That doesn't sound so bad."

"It does to me. The only lawyer I know is Mr. Everhart. Not exactly an inspiration."

"You could be a minister, though."

"Yeah." He grinned again. "But where? I'm half convinced your church is right. And besides, I have a feeling I wouldn't make a very good minister."

He laughed, and so did I. But I'm half convinced he *could* be a good minister someday.

On Sunday, that was two days ago, my family went to Wittemeer one last time. After church, we had dinner with the Meers. Then Annika and Betsie and I spent a final afternoon walking the streets of Wittemeer.

Saying goodbye to them was maybe the hardest thing I've ever done. I know we'll be together again in America, but a year is such a long time. We hugged, and yes, I cried. Some people can go through their whole life and never cry, but I can't be like that.

Speaking of Theo, he chose our last day at the Meers' to argue again that he should stay behind too. It was the same old thing. I have to add stubborn to the list of Theo's faults.

After the evening service, when Mother and Luc and I were all in the wagon ready to go home, Theo was still arguing about it with Father and Uncle Ed. They stood by Uncle Ed's wagon for ten minutes, making us wait. They were too far away for me to hear, but whatever was said, it must have been the right thing, because Theo didn't complain about it on the ride home. And he hasn't complained since.

Early this morning, Mr. Huizen picked us up in his big work wagon and took us to Rotterdam. Mrs. Huizen came along, so she can keep me company on the ride home. She really is the nicest person.

Father sat up front with Mr. Huizen, discussing mostly church things. Mrs. Huizen sat in the back with us. We talked about Rotterdam and sailing ships and America, things we know very little about.

I noticed a small trunk wedged under one of the benches and asked Mrs. Huizen, "What's in the trunk?"

She smiled. "That's a little surprise the widow Wolters asked me to bring along. I'll show you later."

She and Mother resumed their conversation, leaving me to ponder the mysterious trunk. I'll admit, my imagination ran free. Could it be traveling clothes for me? Maybe they planned to announce at the last moment that I could go to America after all.

It was silly to think the widow would be that generous. But still.

When we reached the docks, it was time for more goodbyes. The Meers booked passage on a ship out of Antwerp, so I didn't get to say a final goodbye to Annika. Uncle Ed and Betsie boarded the *Princess Sophia* earlier, so I didn't get a final goodbye with Betsie either.

It's alright. I can't handle any more goodbyes. Mother hugged me like she never wanted to let go. She said, "We love you so much." Then came the final instructions. "Be good for Mrs. Huizen. Help her with the baby. Help her with the house. Don't be any trouble."

Luc wrapped his little arms around my neck so tight I could hardly breathe. "What's trouble?"

Father hugged me too. He had tears in his eyes. I've never seen him cry before. He said, "We'll see you in one year."

Theo hugged me too. He said, "Fourteen months."

So here I stand, alone on the docks in Rotterdam. Well, not alone. Mrs. Huizen is with me. And thousands of others bidding their loved ones goodbye. In some places, people are five and six people deep.

On the *Princess Sophia*, passengers line the railings, but I can't find my family among so many people.

The ship's bells ring out. Sailors in white uniforms glide about the deck, preparing for departure. They raise the sails and cast off the ropes that hold the ship to the dock. The ship drifts out into the current.

Suddenly, I spot Uncle Ed. He stands a head taller than most of the passengers. I jump up and down and wave to him. He sees me and waves back. He's standing beside Father. And there's Mother, holding Luc.

Uncle Ed points toward me, and I wave my arms. Finally, they all see me. They wave and blow kisses. Mother is crying. I'm too far away to see tears, but I can tell by the way she wipes her hand across her cheek.

But where is Theo?

The ship's bells ring again.

I can't find Theo. Did he manage to convince Father to let him stay behind? Is that what they were talking about after church on Sunday night? I told him a hundred times that's a bad idea. Father will need his help in America.

Then I spot him. Not at the rail with the others, but standing on top of a barrel, holding a guide rope. He waves to me, and I wave back.

The ship is moving away now. On its way to America. Tears run down my cheeks. I won't see my family for a whole year. Fourteen months. And no Betsie either.

In a couple of days, I'll return to school, and I don't know how that will go. Will Julia be my friend? What if she's not?

Mrs. Huizen puts her arm around me, and I feel my body tremble. I'm happy for my family. This is best.

We watch until the ship disappears into the distance, then turn back to the wagon. Mr. Huizen is waiting for us. He slides the chest out from under the bench. "And now for your surprise." He opens it wide. It's full of ham and cheese and bread and jam and potatoes and vegetables and four big apple tarts.

I try to seem excited.

He pulls two benches together, forming a sort of table. Mrs. Huizen lays out a tablecloth and sets out four plates. "A picnic lunch, courtesy of the widow Wolters."

I look at the place settings. "Why four?"

She smiles. "We agreed to take another passenger back to Otten with us. I hope you don't mind."

"I don't mind."

Behind the wagon, I hear giggling.

It can't be.

Then a snort-laugh.

It is. "Betsie?"

She squeals with delight and bounces out of hiding.

"What are you doing here? You should be..."

"No," she says. "I shouldn't. I'm staying. With the Huizens. With you."

"But...what about your father? He needs you."

She shakes her head. "He doesn't. It was Theo's idea. A bargain, he called it. A business arrangement. He promised to help my father clear his land this fall and plant crops next spring if he let me stay behind with you."

I don't know what to say.

"Father left the decision to me. I said I want to stay. And it was *my* idea to keep it a surprise. Are you surprised?"

I'm stunned.

We eat our picnic lunch, talking excitedly about what fun we'll have this year. I know I'll miss my family, but right now I'm mostly just thankful. Thankful Betsie is staying with me. Thankful Theo is so stubborn. Thankful for the Huizens. And the Kosters. And the widow Wolters. And especially for God. My refuge in times of trouble.

Later, when Betsie and I are alone in our room in the Huizens' home outside Otten, we talk about the future.

"This will be fun," she assures me. "And even if it's not, it's only a year."

"Fourteen months," I say. "But that's alright. It will give us more time to talk with Julia and the others."

She looks at me. "Talk about what?"

"About coming to church with us. Maybe even America."

"Tess!"

"What? It might happen."

She rolls her eyes. "You're impossible." But then she smiles. "You never give up on your friends."

It's true. It's one of my worst faults.